Book of Common Signs

Book of Common Signs

ASHOK SRINIVASAN

FOURTH ESTATE • *New Delhi*

First published in India by Fourth Estate
An imprint of HarperCollins *Publishers*

Building 10, Tower A, 4th Floor, DLF Cyber City, Phase II,
Gurugram Haryana – 122002, India
www.harpercollins.co.in
2 4 6 8 10 9 7 5 3

P-ISBN: 978-93-5136-161-9
E-ISBN: 978-93-5136-162-6

Typeset in 11.5/14 Dante MT at
SURYA

Printed and bound at
MicroPrints India, New Delhi

Dedicated to the peoples of Palestine, Pakistan,
the Tamils of Sri Lanka and Jews the world over—you who have
borne more than your portion of hard reality,
please share among yourselves this paltry enough
illusion of an illusion

Contents

Not to Be Loose Shunted

PAYLOAD 22.4 / TARE 10.8 / AREA 21.1 /
WHEN EMPTY RETURN TO WADALA

I never knew my father and never saw the sea till I was fourteen years old. My father left us when I was two years old and mother was expecting the second: it was a girl. She was born dead. Later I learnt that mother herself had nearly died giving birth to her. Apart from the wedding photographs (crowds, garlands and fluorescent lights), there is a clear picture of my father taken in his extreme youth: he is standing between a stack of wooden sleepers and a pile of fishplates at a railway level-crossing; he is laughing; you can see the iron tracks meeting at infinity just beyond his hip; black moustache and strong, white teeth. My mother almost never speaks of him.

The only thing about him I know is that he was a very special kind of armchair traveller. He preferred to travel mentally by train, surrounding himself with the latest Bradshaw, maps with broad-gauge, meter-gauge and narrow-gauge markings and issues of the most up-to-date railway timetables. He would make elaborate travel preparations on paper, computing varying costs, allowing for alternative routes, making changes in the itinerary, keeping his options open till the last minute. Actually, he never stirred out of the house. His aversion to travel was matched only by his tireless passion in meticulously plotting the graphs of endless journeys that dovetailed and branched out into still more journeys on paper. I wonder at the names of small railway stations that must have clogged his head. Did he disappear, I wonder, through the shunting yards down some magical cinder track past the railway lines into another life? A fast life composed of coal, steam and iron, not to mention happiness? A place without pain and confusion perhaps?

This game seems to have been necessary and sufficient to absorb his desire for travel. He would make lists of place names along the railroad tracks, catalogues of stations and junctions that would sound like runes or charms to another: Davangere, Kottayam, Lohian Khas, Haldibari, Mariani, Gede and Kolivada. Every person desirous of travelling on a railway shall, upon payment of his fare, be supplied with a ticket specifying the class of carriage for which, and the place from and the place to which, the fare has been paid. My mother was dry-eyed when she told me all this one evening by the sea when I was recuperating from a sudden fever far away from home during the summer holidays. I was then fourteen years old. My parents were both schoolteachers. No one, not even mother, knows why father disappeared for they seemed to have been more than ordinarily happy together. Being a sales representative, I have to travel by train. And the more I travel, no matter what direction I take, the further away I seem to move, mile by iron mile, down the tracks of memory, from the meagre fund of information I possess about my father. The summer I turned fourteen my mother had taken me with her to Vayalur, a village by the sea on the far eastern coast, on a field trip for her research project. We would never have been able to afford the thousand and five hundred miles trip had it not been part of her work.

I saw the sea. We came to it at the end of the last leg of a dusty journey by bus, at the start of which I had begun vomiting. My mother kept looking at me careful not to be caught in her settled habit of watching over me. At the bus depot when I caught my first sight of the sea, I was already burning with fever. I lifted the canvas hold all, quite the young man in control of the situation, stepped down from the bus and without much thought just sat down on the road, after carefully setting down the hold all in the mud.

There was no one on the vast veranda of the local school that evening except my mother and I. My head was cradled in her lap and we both looked out towards the sea that was music to my peevish head. My mother's white sari, I remember, was dramatically splotched with red patches for I had just suffered a nosebleed. Just before the sun went down, I made her take me for a walk on the beach. She spoke to me about her husband, my father, our stranger.

It is a measure of the impact of the sand and salt sea air that I accepted her words about him as the most natural thing in the setting in which they were uttered. Once, my mother's uncle (a sharecropper from the village who had come to town on a matter of land litigation when the stars in the heavens were disposed in his favour) said of my father, what I never really understood: that there was a sort of silence in him that nobody else in the family had, the kind of silence that made rain. I have noticed that people always say such things in times of drought or trouble.

It was not long after mother had retired from teaching. I was staying in Ashok's room (one of a series of wooden cubicles really, over a derelict restaurant in the central market) with his woman, as he was away on tour. Otherwise, Ashok stayed with her and allowed her to earn her own keep when he didn't need her. It was an arrangement we had.

As always, on such occasions, I lied to mother saying I had to go to Kotah on work and would not be back for a week. A mofussil cousin of hers was visiting us and mother planned to take her shopping and show her round town during my proposed absence. One of the water mains down a side street in the city's shopping centre must have burst for the traffic had slowed down at the flooded intersection below.

Ashok's woman and I stood looking out of the window when I suddenly saw my mother looking up at me. She was standing on the curb, her sari raised from the ground, ready to cross the wet street, when she had suddenly looked up and seen me before I was aware of her being there. She covered her mouth in horror and before my aunt could see me, she took her by the elbow and piloted her through the crowd of pedestrians as the lights changed and a fine smell of wet earth as after the first showers of monsoon rose up into the air. She did not mention a word about the matter when I returned home. She has grown quite used to my callous love. She has stopped laughing altogether and does not care for jokes of any kind, so I have taken to teasing her all the more. I told her about the signs in the railway stations, urging the use of Germscutter and the Zinda Tilismath by all travellers, howsoever driven. I told her of the man in the train with a grey caste-mark on his pitted forehead staring at the silently weeping woman on the platform just outside his window as if she were nothing to him. I told her that from Kotah I had been to Bhuswal, Itarsi, Kasbe Sukene, Jaulkhera, Jaisalmer, Burdhwan and Chinchpokhli. The fares shown in these tables are inclusive of the pilgrim/terminal/bridge/municipal/taxes where leviable. But that evening by the sea my mother had made my father unreal to me and I could not sleep that night.

I thought I had a fever that would not go away. I felt profoundly gentle towards and sorry for myself as though some secret store of promise was slowly wasting away within me. My breath came fast and shallow, my lips were dry and my mouth continued to form the necessary, foreign word 'father' again and again. I lay in bed with the ocean loud in my ears. And though I thought I knew him better, my favourite photograph of my father suddenly became cloudy in my eyes.

The next day I had fever again. I had had an early experience with water and now I could not keep my father separate from the sea in my mind. I shut my eyes and immediately I was back on the beach, the wind interfering with my mother's voice talking about him, drowned by the sound of the sea of my fever. On my return home after one of my non-official excursions, she noticed a bite mark on the side of my neck that I myself had not, till then, been aware of. I passed it off as a scratch but she knew better and said nothing. From Vayalur we went on, I remember, to my father's village, to the house in which his parents still lived.

I had never been there before. The main road to the

village bypassed the village and made towards the group of temples that gave the place such local importance as it enjoyed. Seven shrines (not counting those dedicated to spirits meant to ward off cholera, smallpox, plague, locusts), two temples, a vast water tank and five strictly divided lanes constituted a village largely composed of women, children and old men subsisting on an economy of postal money orders. Most of the wells in the villages in that region had gone dry.

We had come to the village close to the end of a longish drought. They had set fire to the dried water hyacinths that choked the bed of the water tank in the centre of the village. This would kill the snakes, clean the tank and provide manure for the paddy fields next season. There were processions in the streets praying for rain. But there was no sign of my father, the rainmaker. There was no sign of any rain—just a few white clouds, empty promises, sailing across the deep blue sky. We stayed there only for two days, long enough for my mother to collect some material from the controlling temple trustees of those parts.

I found even that short stay there awkward. I was weak, but could not sleep at night because of the mosquitoes. My grandparents were very kind to me, but probably felt that I blamed them for their son's having deserted us. I did not know it then but I was never to see them again.

My grandmother, particularly, went out of her way to talk to me about my father: he had run away from home when he was eight years old and was found perched on a tamarind tree the next day. His language, she said, was strong and beautiful, his pauses could not be misconstrued and his silences were as much a part of the man as his words. She was chatting with me as we sat in an angled shaft of sunlight (quick with midges) that shot in from under the thatched canopy over the window. The yellow wash of evening light grew momentarily intense, magically transforming the drab scene outside the window into one of rosy enchantment before subsiding, just as suddenly, into streaks of watery grey.

My grandmother's run-down voice droned on while the house lizards called to each other and the beetles burst against the windowpanes. He ran away from home a second time, she said, when he was thirteen years old. That is one year younger than I was when I heard all this. He was found after a month, wandering in a village thirty miles down the coast: his tongue had grown black in his dry mouth, his words ran into each other and his eyes were dreamy with exhaustion. And even then, my grandmother said, his incoherent words carried within them the clear sounds and motions of sympathy. So he had run away from home twice before he abandoned us. But however hard you run, you can never get away from yourself. If, in addition to all this, you are honest, as his mother said he was, you are truly finished. Better a liar than this honesty on the run. For a man who hated travel so much, my father had certainly travelled distances that took him to places where he could never be reached: he was the presiding absence in our lives.

When we left the village, with that kind of clarity behind us, the water tank was still smoking here and there and the region was rife with rumours of rain. As the train sped away, I remember poking my head out of the railway compartment window and looking back at the parched village we were leaving behind—you never saw such dark, rain-bearing clouds. Years later, the village postmaster kindly wrote to us to say that my grandparents had both died peacefully together in their sleep, as in a story. Recently in my office, the manager said to me in passing that Ashok and I were turning out to be the best reps in the company and that soon our overriding commission would be greater than our basic pay. I have to travel so much that I am rarely home with mother. I can't speak for my mother but it suits me just fine. She waits for me when I am not there and waits on me when I am. I am a travelling salesman and there is work to be done.

One Sunday afternoon I lay in bed smoking a cigarette after lunch and looking out of the window at the blind expanse of the warehouse wall opposite, letting my eyes rest on a part that was perennially wet due to some hidden leakage of water. The black moss had grown thick where the seepage had spread out like a feminine head of hair drying after a bath on a festive morning. Across the street, beyond the gate of the warehouse wall, I could see a truck piled with household furniture crowned with a bicycle, the members of the family standing around, and the servants running back and forth. And suddenly, Srinivasan appeared from behind the lorry carrying a brown paper parcel in his hand. I turned and found my mother standing in the doorway studying me, consuming me with her eyes, in a way she has always done.

Seeing the spell broken she suddenly turned away from me, saying in all innocence, 'You are so much like your father, so much.' Just in time I stopped myself from blurting out something in answer because at this moment she would cry even if I so much as smiled. Thukaithad, Yavatmal, Pollachi, Tenkasi, Panskura, Fazilka and Mankhurd. As a matter of convenience, guards in charge of night mail, express and passenger trains have instructions to awake passengers travelling in the air-conditioned and first classes at any station when requested to do so by passengers in advance. It must be understood however that the railway accepts no responsibility in the matter if passengers oversleep or over-reach their destinations when they are liable to be woken up to the surcharge and penalty.

I was on yet another of my official tours. I could smell the kelp and petrol on the salt sea air long before the train pulled into the station, even before the salt-flats and the marshes appeared quivering over the horizon. The thought occurred to me that my father too must have suffered from the illusion, quite common to all railway passengers, that he was stationary while the world whipped past his window. Of course, in my father's case, this was a reality, for he suffered from a prior illusion that he was a travelling man. It was an illusion within an illusion. Be careful! Don't open that window and look in the direction of your progress or smoke and specks of ash from the railway engine will get into your eyes, not to mention the grit flying in the wind.

Yet another new place, the people speaking a strange language. I booked my suitcase at the left-luggage counter and went into the town. The sky was smudged with smoke and the soft soot drifted down like black snow onto the pedestrians—bent figures who hurried without speech.

Though the place was altogether new to me, at the same time it seemed intimately familiar. The dust-laden wind suddenly picked up, pricking my nostrils and bringing tears to my eyes, while the shopfront awnings and the tarpaulins over the trucks and buses at the inter-state terminal flapped in the wind as though beckoning me, inviting me towards my own lost childhood. I made my rounds, booked the orders and posted the indents.

In the street the ragged children played a game I could not follow. The pressure of unidentifiable familiarity suddenly grew upon me till I felt myself a child, a creature that derives the intent of another's speech without paying heed to the words in which they are bodied forth. Bewildered and depleted I returned to the railway station and dozed off in the retiring room. It was dark when I woke up.

At that hour of the night the station seemed deserted. The tea stall was closed, a porter lay motionless on his angled handcart on the opposite platform. Two dogs and a cow were sleeping at the foot of the overbridge and an old man was retching under an iron tap at the far end of the platform. Outside, in the general darkness of the silent buildings, there were a few oblongs and parallelograms of yellow light. I walked on. A dog was kicked out of a restaurant whose rolling shutters were being pulled down. With a parched throat I parted the bead curtain and entered her cubicle in the brothel and found her asleep. She woke up for me with burning eyes. I lay amidst her exhausted limbs without slaking my thirst. Quilon, Jersaguda, Nasik, Pathankot, Monghyr, Raxaul and Masjid. The railway will not be responsible for any loss, deterioration or damage that may occur to luggage, unless the same has been duly booked and proper charges paid thereon to the concerned authorities, nor are they responsible for booked articles in charge of irresponsible owners.

Such passengers, should they be holding first-class tickets, are recommended to leave a servant inside their compartment to guard their property whilst they are absent in the refreshment room, bathroom or dining car, but this can only be done if the compartment is otherwise unoccupied or occupied by like-minded passengers who can take turns with your servant while you take turns with theirs. In the last dark of early morning, I left the brothel, without having entered her sleep or dreams, for the half-light of the bug-infested retiring room above the railway station.

The light bulb burned dimly in its locked wire cage in the station lavatory. The separate feathers of a rotting broom lay floating in the ooze of the waterlogged urinal before me as I recalled a childhood train ride with my maternal grandmother in the monsoons through the Ghats: seeing the swollen watercourses in the hills my grandmother had said, 'Close up, you will find the water filthy', and we had laughed. Even the rocky patches gave off a healing smell of rain-sodden, crushed herbs. Otherwise, for the most part, you could see the dripping and fragrant countryside of sweet-smelling scrub, dissected here and there by gullies of white rain water from the hills with their different shades of tender green. Uluberia, Titagarh, Alwaye, Lalgola, Dadar, Sodepur, Dankuni . . .

The Light, the Way

Since nothing is more auspicious than the presence of an only son and his only son at the funeral pyre, Ishan and his father were suddenly faced with a journey almost halfway round the world.

Ishan's grandfather, who was dying, had stopped writing letters a year ago. The last few letters—he was a meticulous correspondent in the vernacular—complained of eye trouble and his anxiety about some journey into the interior. One night, when Ishan returned home late from Linda, his father was waiting up for him with a letter in his hand informing them that the old man was slowly but steadily sinking.

Pieced together from many letters and translated by his father, Ishan learnt of his grandfather's strange eye problem. Like watermarks stamped into paper, worms of light, in the shape of three links of a bicycle chain—those pure creatures of an effulgent reality—wriggled before his eyes without impairing his sight and drifted from the lower boundary of his vision towards the upper margin. At the exact moment of their disappearance, they reappeared below and followed their fixed and unvarying course upwards. They did not impede his sight or cause him any pain or physical irritation. Rather, they were a beautiful distraction superimposed on all he saw. His handwriting worsened while the content of his letters grew in grace and lucidity but proceeded to a point beyond comprehension. This was later to develop into a strange condition which forced him to see the past, the present and the future simultaneously, as though in him the compound eyes of an insect were turned from viewing space to time. Did he perhaps look inwards because of this? Was this the journey into the interior he referred to? Was he reduced to total silence because of something he saw within himself? It was difficult to understand why a man of his age suddenly wanted to travel, and it was completely unclear where he wanted to go.

When the letters stopped coming a year ago, news came via friends, relatives and even strangers, some of whom became friends on the strength of the reports they brought of the old man in Kanjivai, the ancestral village in the Cauvery delta on the north-western seacoast. In that short period, the old man had become a religious leader to whom miraculous cures were attributed. God knows there were omens and signs enough.

Unknown rains fell upon the rocky, arid regions south-east of Kanjivai and some weeks later, the desert blossomed with whole meadows of young grasshoppers which, through constant body contact, changed colour, turned cannibalistic and took to the air, laying waste the countryside. Iridescent as a mica storm in the pitiless sunlight, cloud upon cloud of orange-and-black locusts, their green innocence gone, denuded the villages in their blind path of hunger.

While news of this dreadful visitation was on everyone's lips, word spread around Kanjivai that a leper who was begging from door to door was suddenly made clean and whole when he appeared before the door of Ishan's grandfather's house. At this juncture, all the bamboo-stands in Kanjivai—in the world, actually—began to flower.

This was something that had never happened in living memory. After its full flowering and before the bamboo clumps died, rats swarmed through the thickets devouring the bamboo fruit. Town and village alike were ravaged by the plague. Numberless callers arrived at the old man's house. It was reported that even victims of the plague survived merely by passing before his door.

While a few surviving bamboo rhizomes in his backyard put out weak pencils of culms that would take more than a decade to attain their full former maturity, a gnarled dead tree before the veranda of his house began to glow at night with a secret light. By day it was home to termite and fungus. The emission of this heatless light drew swarms of fireflies that settled on the twisted branches of the leafless tree; and as the light emitted by the fireflies became synchronous, an awesome hush fell upon the sea of expectant faces, broken by the simultaneous pealing of all the temple bells in the area.

While the sound vibrated and died upon the humid air, all the lights in Kanjivai were doused for a minute, plunging the town into complete darkness, leaving the lone tree glowing with fairy lights. And though there were not people enough to count the dead, whole hosts of the faithful prayed to the blind seer as to a living saint. The old man gave no discourses and performed no rituals. He lay speechless on a string cot on the veranda of the ancient house where he had been born, and people flocked to see him. It was enough to see him lying there, with his head turned away perhaps, barely drawing breath, to effect the most fantastic cures in the pressing multitudes. Even letters sent to him, unanswered, unopened even, worked wonders through the Indian postal system.

He was regarded as the greatest practitioner of the healer's art. A vast organization of the faithful, to which the old man was totally indifferent, sprang up around him to handle the mail, the concourse of supplicants and all the necessary arrangements to marshal the traffic of millions of cripples, believers and incurables. There were additional trains to Thalayut, the station nearest to Kanjivai, called Pilgrimage Specials. The drowsy village had become a booming town—expensive, chaotic and holy. They said the old man was saintly. They said he was mad. The people adored him. The people reviled him. He was seer. He was a fake. A healer. A charlatan. God. Fraud.

Ishan, at nineteen years of age, was a disappointment to his father, who, like his father and forefathers before him, worked with vegetable dyes on coarse cotton, painting detailed and repetitive pictures of multi-armed goddesses in strict accordance with traditional values, to be used as wall-hangings in prayer rooms. Ishan did not continue the family tradition, but worked for a photographer's studio attached to a press-cum-bindery, in Soho. He was involved in the production of special, limited editions of candid camerawork in hard-core pornography exclusively for circulation to members of private clubs. His people knew nothing about it.

Ishan's father considered each of his own unsigned,

anonymous productions a work of art, simply because in colour values and the relationship of lines to planes, each picture faithfully re-created an earlier picture through the exact reproduction in line and colour, not of the model, but of what he had learned of the religious texts from his father. For generations the family had stuck to paintings of the four forms of the goddess Parvati as they obtained in Madurai, Kanchipuram, Nagapattinam and Varanasi: Meenakshi, Kamakshi, Neelayadhakshi and Vishalakshi.

And though nobody considered them works of art, Ishan's father sold a great number of his cloth paintings at modest prices to members of the immigrant community there. As an artisan he always referred to his craft as art. For him, a work of art by an artist must be unique in its total congruence with that of his predecessor without being, in any way, a copy of it.

All true pictures of the goddess were the same and no two pictures were ever the same. He spoke often with contempt of Ashok, a sculptor of temple deities in the home country who went commercial, gave up the ways of his forefathers and took to fashioning nudes and fountains in garden settings. Later, Ashok was reduced to hacking granite into millstones for grinding meal and moonlighting as a stonemason to scratch a meagre living for himself. In his own shy, unspoken way, he was proud of his son's poor English gleaned from a nearby county school and did his best to hide his hurt about Ishan's ignorance of Tamil and temple painting. He often spoke to Ishan about their family, the village they came from and his own remembered childhood. He read him excerpts from the scriptures and told him stories of myths culled from the epics, which he himself had been told when young. In return, Ishan never mentioned a word about his own job, what it involved and where it led him, for he was happy in his own work and more than a little ashamed of his father. India may have been his father's country but it was not his. Not discounting the limescale orthodoxy of his Hindu upbringing, it was here, amid the pubs, the pawn shops and the football pools that he had grown up to man's estate, on forbidden fish and chips and with the recession and the cruise missiles looming before him.

His father would switch off the telly, sit on the carpet before the fire with the weighty family album before him and point out various figures to Ishan, telling him their names and histories. As often as not, Ishan's mind strayed into the red darkness of his studio where Linda had first shown him unexpected kindness. The strange names and half-familiar faces photographed in foreign places never remained welded for long in Ishan's mind, and so it became a pleasant and chatty winter evening exercise with the family that would bear endless repetition. The album was not only a prized family possession to which each generation had added its pictures, but a holy article used in ancestor worship.

Ishan was numbed by the detailed and wordy delineation of the family tree, replete with formally posed photographs of other people with hints of a likeness to himself. The four corners of the album were touched with auspicious vermilion. With unseeing eyes Ishan gazed at the album, at the pictures of his grandaunts and great-granduncles, in formal poses and stiff postures with stern faces.

Preparations for their return home were going apace when news arrived of the old man's death. Things were completed in an altered mood and tempo, full of reminiscences and new orthodoxies. While they were waiting to leave for the airport, unannounced friends who had heard of the blind man's passing away in India dropped by directly from Heathrow to speak to Ishan's father.

After serving them tea, Ishan's mother withdrew into the kitchen with tears in her eyes but returned dry-eyed in the doorway, the better to take in the latest gossip. The few words spoken issued out of a comfortably shared silence that was to prepare Ishan for the things that would need saying or be left unsaid on his first journey to the land of his forefathers.

'Will it be four days then?'

'About. It is the heat I am afraid of. For him.' The old man nodded towards Ishan.

'How many years since you went there?'

'Twenty-five years. I remember like it was yesterday; I was reluctant to leave India for England then as I am reluctant now to make the journey in reverse.'

'Things have changed, you know? The old routes are not open any more and new connections and detours are now operative.'

'There are special trains to Thalayut Junction now and one does not have to wait for the weekly boat-train. What, I say! The buses and autos have now replaced the bullock carts and rickshaws to Kanjivai. Jokes apart, you cannot recognize Kanjivai now. Things are not what they were.'

'Don't go by what you remember. Ask at every point what direction and mode of transport you should take. Though I must say, I don't think any of this will apply to you as your arrival there is expected. You will be escorted on the last lap of your journey. Your father was an extraordinary man.'

'The last words he was heard to murmur before his death

were: "So long ago, these memories, they seem to belong to an earlier birth of mine."'

'He died as he lived, without having acquired any possessions, but seeing that body peacefully waiting for death, nobody could have thought it had ever known want.'

'He was as luminous as only a man who has not wronged his brethren might be at the moment of dying.'

'The night he died the Cauvery caught fire. The river burned and burned for miles, from the estuary halfway up to Srikakulam.

'The newspapers carried stories the next day that the industrial wastes and pollutants from the factories and oil refineries upriver had caused the fire, but the people would have none of that. They repeated the story umpteen times; I ask you, brother, even if that were so, why did the river catch fire that night? Can anyone answer me that? The people are not fools. I told that ass of a journalist, it won't wash, my boy! It simply won't wash! How can anybody ask the people not to believe what they see with their own eyes?'

When one of the visitors said, 'They are waiting for both of you', everybody present was suddenly recalled from considering the old man's piety to the fact of his death. In the silence that followed, some sipped the cold dregs of the tea spiced with lemon grass and ginger.

'Ashok is finished now. You may have heard. The crows had been at him all day long when his body was found in an abandoned granite quarry. They had been searching for him for three days; they had been finding him everywhere. I was told the southern side of the temple's gopuram remains incomplete to this day. Poor chap, he'd been asking for it for donkey's years and when it came he was not ready for it.

He's finished; I told him long ago he'd never get a bite fishing in the puddle of his own piss, but would be listen? Poor fellow, he's finished—simply finished!'

There were smiles at this irrelevancy. The mood lightened perceptibly and one of them launched into a lengthy anecdote about Srinivasan, a distant uncle of Ishan's. 'Even Srinivasan has come to the end of his rope—Srinivasan who was as meek as a mouth-less insect. It is so funny you won't believe it! When they brought Srinivasan home from the office, he was perorating on how exactly a man may get to the interstate bus terminus. His clearly enunciated words were already a mix of geography and the sacred shastras: 'After the esplanade on the left you must move straight on beyond all attachment and desire till you arrive at the coal depot outside the old customs office . . .'

For two days and three nights, Srinivasan's increasingly hoarse voice could be continuously heard giving non-stop directions that no human being could possibly follow. Unimpeded by the rumoured whispers of those around him, Srinivasan's steady, dry voice kept detailing the topography of the city as though he would exhaust the grammar of his existence along the narrow by-lanes and gullies running between the compound walls of shuttered bungalows with their courtyards open to the sky, all marked by the daily wash hung out to dry.

Quite simply, what had happened was this: a man, a foreigner, had come up to Srinivasan in the office asking for directions to get to the interstate bus terminus. Srinivasan gave him the most detailed, uncalled for and literally interminable directions on the many likely routes he should not be seduced by if he hoped to reach his destination by the quickest possible path.

'Do you know where Kurla is?' asked Srinivasan.

'No,' said the man, standing in front of him with the tips of his fingers playing along the edge of the table.

'All right. Sit down, please. You know where Ghatkopar station is?'

'Yes.'

'Good. You catch your tram in front of the railway station, number 23. It will take you straight to Nagpada Chowk. You get down there and walk straight on. Are you following me?'

'Thank you,' said the stranger. 'Yes.'

'You want to take the first turning on you right at Nagpada Chowk itself and ignore the first two streets on your left. Go straight on till you see a clock tower on your right. Stop me if I am going too fast. Till what on your right?'

'Clock tower,' said the man, suppressing a smile and already looking tired.

'Right,' said Srinivasan and hit the table with the palm of his hand. 'After you pass the clock tower on your right, take the first turning on the left and keep straight on till you come to a domed red-brick building. Till what building? That's right: a domed red-brick building. It's unmistakable. But that is not the building you want. What you should do is leave the building after the domed red-brick building and take the second one in the same line further on. If you enter by the exit gate marked `No Entry', you will find yourself facing the annexe. This is a short cut, I am telling you. You go through the annexe, jump over the compound wall and walk across the Gandha Nullah before cutting across the maidan . . .'

When the stranger suggested he would take a taxi or scooter, Srinivasan implored him not to waste his money on scooters and taxis, which would certainly take the most circuitous routes to increase their fares. 'Want not, waste not,' said Srinivasan to the harassed foreigner and suggested that he take down in writing the directions given by him. When the foreigner, full of resolution, took a few steps towards the door, Srinivasan sprang up and physically tried to detain him. His colleagues intervened, and so matters were sorted out.

Srinivasan's speech wound down, in the insane asylum, to disconnected phrases and words. The pauses between sentences, then between phrases and finally between words grew longer and longer till he fell silent of his own accord. The visitor ended the story with the words, 'It was so funny, I can't tell you.' The visitors departed amid small laughter and good cheer. Ishan understood each separate word well enough but the significance of the wholly pointless digression quite eluded him. He had to be content with the thought that he would soon see for himself the country they endlessly referred to.

The journey itself was nothing, less than nothing. Mosquitoes, heatstroke and diarrhoea lent their passage to India the quality of a dream. There was no cremation, for the body, un-iced and un-embalmed, showed no signs of decay, giving off instead a mild fragrance of jasmine into the humid air of the tropics: the incorruptible body now belonged less to the family than to the faithful and it was now well on the way to joining the pantheon of Indian gods.

It was already winter when father and son returned home from home, with their separate, unshared assumptions intact, though shaken. They returned cicatrized with half-remembered bits and pieces that did not fit each other and were incongruous with the facts of their journey. The first snow of the winter that had thawed into muddy puddles earlier in the day had by evening, hardened into drifts of dirty ice again. As Ishan lay in bed, solarized images of his nightmare journey ate like quicklime into the flesh of his sleep: diazo memories in patches kept him awake all night, such as his first sight of the glassy airport undulating in the heat haze; a crowd of people on the edge of a vast maidan gathered around a young woman possessed by spirits after accepting buttermilk in a coconut shell from a stranger; his grandfather's house: the front veranda, the cavernous hall (with dead leaves rattling in the corners) opening directly on to the large backyard enclosed by a high earthwork wall; and there, beyond the water-well and young bamboo clumps, the roofless lavatory in the far corner, cicada-loud and full of the black berries of the curry-leaf tree outside. Like that far-off house, his father too would soon become a derelict—a human shell fitted out with beliefs that nowhere and in no way meshed with the common cams and gears of the technology of the day. It was still dark outside and the sodium street lamps cast an orange glow through the freezing fog. Tears sprang to Ishan's eyes, not because Linda was gone or his grandfather dead but because he now knew that the time had come for him to leave home.

Whale Song

It is the very end of the monsoons. But it's raining still. It is a bad time of the year to move house and that too into the suburbs of a new city. After Jaisalmer and the other small, desert towns of Rajasthan, Mumbai in the monsoon season is a new experience for Ishan. No burning wind or sand dunes here in this flooded backwater of the city.

Ishan is standing on the back veranda and staring at the derelict building opposite, which looks like it might be a haunted house melting in the wet. At nine years of age, Ishan feels a vague sense of new possibilities opening up. But what of the loss of familiar faces and places? It is part of growing up and moving on. There is the quickening expectation that he may even hope to out-distance the dark shadows of childhood.

Ishan's father, Dwaraka Nathan Kara, a cloth merchant, has been forced to make this move from Jaisalmer to the suburbs of Mumbai for business reasons. Ishan's mother, Kamala, does not think so much as hope that things will improve: after the sun and sand of Jaisalmer, these city clouds seem to be raining into her very soul. Kamala's younger and as yet unmarried sister, Gauri, simply wants the geographical change to change her whole life for the better. Dwaraka's blind, widowed mother, who sees all, knows that this big move is only a form of rebirth, a new place where old accounts will be settled.

The men are moving the furniture into the new house. The floor is streaked with mud and slush. The men are shouting to each other. The house itself is newish, but decidedly old-fashioned with an enclosed courtyard in the middle and a back veranda, which opens out on to a thorny cinder patch in the middle of which stands the half-built building with blind windows, banisterless staircases and discontinuous, exposed plumbing.

Ishan finds this abandoned building far more interesting than the new house they are moving into; it seems as if out of every gaping window and door-less doorway, new friends will jump out to welcome him. Pigeons have taken over the whole rainy building. Grass and peepal trees grow out of the cracks and drainpipe junctions. Time and termites have taken their toll on the windowsills and doorframes. Rusting tar drums and thorn trees surround the place. Some rowdies are throwing stones at the building from the middle distance. And beyond them lie the iridescent saltpans and then nothing but the marsh leading to the sea. It's a flat horizon.

Ishan turns and goes into the house. He stops inside the threshold of the backroom because of Gauri and Dwaraka. Gauri and Dwaraka are not close enough to touch each other. They are not talking to each other when Ishan enters the room; nor is there the pause that follows something spoken between two people. But out of the congealed silence grows the fine flower of complicity that binds both figures in a tableau of sexual conspiracy. Caught in a private moment they are eyeless, their separate selves dissolving in a common pool between themselves. Their faces are closed and they are absent where they stand. Gauri's face is turned towards Ishan but she is wholly unaware of him. In that rainy light, all the world has lost definition in her eyes but the figure of Dwaraka before her. And Dwaraka with his back to Ishan seems to be waiting—waiting and unable to turn or turn away. Ishan feels but does not understand the heavy stillness in the air. It is only for a moment—but it seems endless—that all three of them are caught and held together. Ishan breaks the frozen spell by moving past them into the house. The wet pieces of furniture are still coming in.

Ishan concentrates on the men moving the stuff into the house. His blind grandmother, surrounded by all the household junk, is calmly busy with her extraordinary work of embroidery: appliqué work where she seems to be able to smell the colours of the patches and threads. Her work is beautiful beyond imagination or belief. As his eyes come to rest on her, the small slight frame of his body acquires a sudden stillness that is promptly shattered by his mother's voice, 'Dwaraka, there are ants in the toilet.'

'You and your unending complaints,' his father says.

'It's only a sign of diabetes,' the grandmother says reassuringly. 'It is the waste sugar that the ants go for.'

In order to distract herself, his mother calls to him, 'Ishan, Ishan. Now where's that boy?' Her voice already heavy with the hint of tears, trails off without conviction.

'Leave him alone,' his father says with the static of disgust crackling in his voice. 'He's nine years old and always sneaking around listening to the elders. If you stop tying him to your sari, he'll stop pussyfooting around and grow up into a man.'

There is the usual exchange of words that mark the beginning of the old pattern of the conjugal fight. Dark on dark, the quarrel takes familiar shape behind Ishan's back.

'Do you think I am blind like your mother? Do you really think I do not know what is going on? Look at how you've been brought up. And you, trying to teach me how to bring up our son.'

'Shut your mouth. A good example you're setting him screaming at your husband like this.'

'You are a good one to speak of examples—with a father like you he's finished anyway.' She falls to weeping and breaks apart. If it's not the enormity of what she's just said, it's the dead weight of what she suspects she knows. Also, this is merely a pause in the old slanging match; and Ishan, his face wet from the rain, recognizes it as such. Gauri is nowhere to be seen.

'Look at you. You've changed so much. You are not the same person I married any more. Now you take me wholly for granted. I don't mind that—it's the complete lack of tenderness, because the relationship is dead. What am I that I am reduced to looking to you for even a hint of an assurance, which normally should be given naturally without my having to ask for it. You come to me with the shut face of a stranger. Just look at you . . .' It will go on like this and already the light in the sky is failing.

It is daylight. It is dazzling. The lorry and movers are long gone. A marginal degree of order has been restored at home. Ishan is in the ground floor of the derelict building. His feet are wet through and through. Outside, he can see a group of ragged urchins clutching stones in their hands, conspiring. All around them are puddles of water reflecting the sky like so many shards of a shattered mirror. Yesterday there were only three hooligans. Today there are five of them. There is some writing on a part of the wall that has been plastered. It is the work of many hands. There is no order, by way of sequence or continuity in the entries:

Silence is golden. All men are brothers.
No spitting. Rice plate ready.
Management not responsible for lost property.
Anything extra—extra. All women are sisters.
Fixed price. No bargaining. No credit.
Outside eatables not allowed.
No sitting for long allowed.
Milk not for sale. Toned milk used here.
Please do not whistle. Please do not comb.
All men and women are not brothers and sisters.

There is an excited babble outside the half-built pile: the dispossessed street children are vandalizing the half-built hallway on the other side of the building. From an overhang, rusty iron rods stick out of the reinforced concrete; and the boys take turns pulling them down by swinging on them. One of them ties a dead cat to a rod by a length of hemp while another uses it as a target to throw stones at. Ishan resolves to return later and look into the other rooms.

It is afternoon. Ishan takes stock of the silent building and the lengthening shadows in corners. In spite or because of the rain, the light in the washed-out sky is unsettling. Ishan hears whispers from another room, veined with his father's low voice kept down to breathing level. Ishan walks up the staircase, his eyes full of other rooms on other floors. There are no banisters and the gaping stairwell is ringed with iron rods sticking out of the stony concrete. On the fourth floor, the landing is particularly crowded with broken pipes, empty tar drums and heaps of disintegrating bricks. He walks down the long, half-built corridor towards the rooms on the far side and looks out over the unprotected balcony: eight ruffians are roasting pigeons over a fire. They are eating away and a large number of dead birds lie beside them. A strong smell of roasting flesh and burnt feathers rises up. The sky and land meet in a hazy, grey horizon and Ishan sees Gauri quickly slinking out of the side of the building with furtive steps.

For no very clear reason that he can think of, Ishan steps back into the shadow of the doorway and sings the school morning-assembly song:

Father, we thank thee for the night
And for the blessed morning light . . .

He sings at the top of his voice and stops short after the first two lines. He walks up to the terrace of the building over the seventh floor, and surprises a sudden cloud of pigeons that burst into the rainy sky.

There is no surrounding wall, no debris as on the other floors. Nothing impedes the eye except the wet figure of Dwaraka who stands with his back to the edge, facing Ishan with the look of a trapped, wild animal in his eyes. Something is terribly wrong with his father's face, contorted to the point of being unrecognizable. He is wearing the closed face of a stranger.

Ishan walks up to him. His father does not look away or turn aside. Not a word is spoken; he merely takes a few steps backwards till he's poised on the very edge of the building: he has become insubstantial, airy and almost translucent. Ishan comes up to him and places the palm of his right hand on Dwaraka's midriff.

His father waits for the push because he needs an excuse. And Ishan in order to complete what his father began must push him before he turns transparent and shatters like glass. Ishan gives him a push and before his unbelieving eyes, his father bends backwards and topples into the evening. He falls endlessly through the falling rain and lands at last not far from where the boys are gathered round the fire. They scatter in all directions. The pigeons boomerang back to their roosts. Ishan stands rooted in the rain.

It is the third doctor and four years later. Ishan has not spoken a word since his father's death. He attends a special school for the mute and sees a therapist thrice a week. Therapists talk. But it means nothing. Often enough they talk as if they are looking to cure themselves of some secret malaise that's killing them. It does not help Ishan any, but he listens. If he were to speak out, the therapist would shut up and listen from the safety of his distanced silence. And then, who would understand what Ishan has to say? No one understands Ishan like his disintegrating grandmother.

The once derelict building has since been completely vandalized and gutted by fire. The surrounding houses, including Ishan's, bear the indelible marks of its going up in smoke. Kamala and Gauri—now locked together with several ties like shared childhoods, attachment to a common absence and separate memories of love/hate—have taken over the shop and made a spectacular success of it. One of the prize items they deal in is the grandmother's embroidery.

From the day Dwaraka died, Ishan's grandmother began to forget things. In her embroidery she begins a pattern, forgets how to proceed, and repeats the same or some other beginning and so on. But the end result is, if that is possible, even more beautiful than her earlier works. In this way she hides her eroding memory from the others who see her every slip as a new departure on her part. As a child growing up in the deserts of Jaisalmer, she had been told a story about some singing whales that lived round about the snowy wastes of Alaska but travelled thousands of miles past icebergs, coral reefs and atolls to commit mass suicide on the sands of some palmy beach in the tropics. She is a child of the desert sands of Rajasthan. She has never seen the sea. She has never seen snow. She is haunted by this image of pods of whales giving vent to euphonic bursts of sublime melody in their eurhythmic passage past peninsulas and archipelagos, finding their way, in ways we will never understand, to their final resting place. She is deeply moved by their mysterious movements in that vast body of salty water. Every snatch of whale song is yet another movement in a natural composition that propels them from their icy deserts to a sandy end. All her life she has dreamed of those icebergs; she sincerely believes that her work of embroidery is something like the reefs and atolls built by corals. In her mind's eye she sees lunar caverns picked out in a patchwork of submarine lights, fringed by waving fronds; increasingly she is haunted by the shadows of the passing whales and she strains every fibre of her being to listen to their distant, inhuman music.

Earlier, only certain rhapsodic movements of the whale's death song reached her. But now she has made the entire symphony her own. She sees in her mind's eye that whole areas of her past are crumbling and slipping from her like parts of an icy mainland breaking away and drifting off as icebergs into the sea of forgetfulness. But nobody knows, nobody suspects. Her only son is dead, and the whale song that was a rare whisper in the eustachian tubes of her ear is loud and clear these days. She calls Ishan to her. She is sitting cross-legged on a reed mat in her corner of the room and Ishan lies down with his head in her lap. She runs her fingers through his hair and tells him, for the umpteenth time, the story of the whale song that her grandmother had told her. He understands as never before that she is losing her memory. The person closest to him is divesting herself of her past.

She tells him also that she heard the story from her grandmother as a child. That afternoon—it is a Sunday—Ishan sets fire to his school. He does not know that it is he who has set fire to the school. Perhaps it was he who had set fire to the derelict building next door. It is only much later, after many fires, that he will understand the terrible power of his silence. The next day he goes to school as usual. And all he sees are police cordons, firefighters, flashing lights and the black, smoking debris behind the crowds held at bay. The new doctor promises to be no better than the earlier ones. Only this one professes to place no faith in medicines. He is a devout man, wedded to the belief that patient and doctor, in connivance with God, can sort out this and all other problems.

Locked in perpetual silence himself Ishan grows up friendless. It is now eleven fires and twelve years after his father's death and he is quite used to his solitary condition. Ishan still does not know that it is he who started these fires by dreaming of them in his sleep and forgetting about them on waking up. His grandmother, completely bereft of her memory, lies in her corner like a discarded broom or a beached whale. She speaks only to Ishan and he listens only to her. All her talk is of whales and water. At her funeral pyre, when her body catches fire of its own accord, he recalls in complete detail his dream of the night before, and understands for the first time how he had started all the other fires and so released from his long silence he calls out to his long dead father.

Time and Again

School had just given over and Ishan, Lila and Ajit took the shortcut to the Trombay Hills through the new housing development beyond the golf links and the Old Sindhi Colony. They were making plans about the movies they were going to see. As they walked through the dust storm Ishan thought back briefly to the movie he had seen with Lila two weeks earlier: *The Return of the Son of Part Two Revisited*. In the darkened theatre she had whispered something to Ishan which he couldn't quite catch, the vague thrilling words made vibrant by the fact of her hair and breath on his ear. The temperature was 45 degrees in the shade. It was the worst time of the year. That year the monsoons had not yet broken. There was a heat wave on, the papers said. Earlier in the day, during the long recess, Vittal had told Ishan that he had seen a bird fall dead from a tree before his very eyes. The exams were at an end and the holidays were not very far off. A new mood of reckless happiness was loosed upon the school. Everything tasted better—even the blade of grass scorched to yellow straw. All were carried away by the same sense of carefree foolishness coursing through their blood. The oddly assorted threesome walked on, for the sun however fierce was young to them—so completely absorbed were they in the exciting intimacy of their discussion. It was a bald, treeless colony where at noon it would be impossible to find a shadow the size of a human being.

'I don't believe that Ajit,' said Lila. 'When I first learnt about it, I could never believe it of my parents. Actually I woke up crying in the middle of the night and my brother Ashraf put on the light and my sister Zarina talked me into going back to sleep before grandmother woke up. Jamil went on sleeping, as usual. Oh God, how I cried.'

'It was Denzil who first explained it to me,' said Ishan. 'We had been playing Seventiles, but it had got too dark to continue with the game and we stood around the stone culvert talking in a group, waiting till one of us was called away by an adult, which was the general signal for us to break up when Denzil, who was older, asked me, 'Aye, do you suffer from night-loss?' I said, I didn't know and the others laughed and Pervez said to Denzil, 'Oh, leave him alone.' But Denzil went on with a smile on his face, 'Do you know that one drop of spunk is equal to thirty-two drops of blood? Look at that Dilip with his chest all caved-in, completely shagged out.' They laughed again, forgot all about me and went on talking among themselves . . .' The dust storm was coming to an end amid the shuttered buildings baking blind in the sun which appeared as a white disc in the dust haze.

Ajit agreed to stay below at the lower reaches of the foothills and alert them if he saw anybody coming. The place was truly deserted, enveloping them in the breathless furnace of silence composed of insect noises. Stranded in time, Ishan and Lila took their first steps up the hill between the crags and thorn trees. Between the bald rocks breathing fire grew strange, spiky scrubs. The way forward seemed impossible but they pushed through between the brambles to yet more boulders and nettles. They did not know how long they had been up in the hills when the air suddenly gave off the scent of hard rain on parched earth.

They pursued their way through a gully of huge, smooth pebbles screened by prickly bushes until, suddenly, like a revelation, they came upon a secret body of sweet, still water among the rocks: a tarnished mirror with the hot blue sky pulsing above. 'I wish I had my camera with me,' said Lila. They did not know how long they played around in the water or how they found their way out and down (in soft focus and slow motion) to the foothills. That night Lila came down with a fever which disappeared by morning. The word spread through the school and both, Lila and Ishan, were regarded with a new interest by the juniors. 'It was just like in the movies,' Lila said. Some of the new boys came up to Ishan in the recess with a shy question or two. Ashraf turned away from him with a sullen resentment in his eyes. When Joshua, a senior, asked him about it, Ishan shrugged off the incident with the comment, 'Oh, Lila is just movie-mad.'

Later, standing round the stone culvert on the street corner of the housing estate where several of the boys lived, Ishan waved aside the whole thing. 'Though we had great difficulty in finding our way back, we had a good swim,' he said. 'She laughed a lot. I laughed—it was wonderful.' Later he said, 'I hope we can find that place again. It's the greatest place for a swim. Clear sweet water hidden away in the hills.' He half-closed his eyes in ecstasy and kissed the tips of his fingers. 'His new maanja's fantastic! No kite within his reach will ever be reeled in.' 'That is nothing; have you seen the new catty Shanky's made from a guava-vee? Man, seven bloodsuckers in one day.' 'Swimming in the Govandi well is possible only in the monsoons.' 'Then why didn't he come for the swim.' 'Don't be funny—you must be mad.' 'He lost his scapular.' 'He's always cribbing about something or the other.' 'Forget it.'

At the beginning of the next term, when Ishan's grandmother passed away, Jamil said, 'I wish it had been my grandmother,' and both Zarina and Lila said, 'Shh! you must not say things like that'; and, 'Shh! Don't say that.' All the four children detested their cruel grandmother. Ishan and his friends made several trips to the hills but they could never again locate that pool of secret water among the rocks.

Over the years, the hills themselves were steadily bulldozed out of existence to make way for the vast oil refinery complex, the fertilizer plants and the atomic energy establishment. By the time these marks of technological progress had come into being—issuing smoke and casting a rosy glow for miles around the night sky of the city—Ishan and all his friends were dispersed. Darius was in America, Pervez was dead and Denzil was stuck in Russia; Joshua who was planning on emigrating to Australia had ended up in Israel. Ishan himself (with his wife and two children) was now located in Delhi. He learned indirectly that Lila had relocated; there were other stories that she had done a course in photography, that she was teaching school. He had returned once to Mumbai, years ago, but there was none of the old crowd left. People sat at home and watched television and the old movie-houses

(Metro, New Empire, Excelsior, Eros, Regal, Bijoux, Radio City . . .) had become empty echo-chambers like the temples in the villages: good for bats, and nothing else.

Ishan had already risen to the rank of Organizer in the powerful Association of Cloth Mills Combine. It was a job that had its undesirable aspects but Ishan was getting used to it. The Organizers of the Combine toured the country and filed their reports; based on their reports the Combine would decide which mills needed closing down. For the mill-hands, the very appearance of an Organizer of the ACMC on the scene was an evil omen that spelled retrenchment, closure, lockout and the useless promise of the setting up of power-looms in another part of the country. Still, Ishan Kara had done well so far. As he was setting out for Jasool, news came in that another Organizer had disappeared under suspicious circumstances while on duty in the western region; the crows and stray dogs had been at his decapitated body rotting near the sewage treatment plant. Another Organizer of the ACMC was crucified on an anthill in a cantonment town on the eastern seaboard. There were rumours about a third Organizer who was missing—he had joined an anarchist group dedicated to the violent overthrow of the Combine; it was the worst time of the year. As the train, breathing fire, was shunted into a siding, Ishan looked out into the blinding glare of the afternoon just in time to see a mynah fall dead from a neem tree opposite his coach. It was an endless stretch of rocky country scarred by gullies and thorn trees.

And Ishan thought how once when he was in Nasik on work he had, on an impulse, walked into a college canteen only because the entrance to the adjoining movie-house was through the canteen. There were a few boys and girls discussing movies; he had raised his eyes from his teacup and looked in astonishment at the girl in an indigo sari—but it was not Lila.

Ishan was travelling towards Jasool, a place he had never been to before. The monsoon had not yet broken and the temperature was 45 degrees in the shade. There was a heat wave on, the papers said. As the train hurtled through the hot night, he could see the small forest fires in the surrounding hills: the black shapes of the burning trees behind the orange fires sending up an occasional spray of sparks. In Jasool, when Ishan first saw Lila, she and another teacher with a large group of schoolgirls were filing past an enormous cinema hoarding. They came towards him as he stood there in the shadow, waiting for them. The girls were all singing, laughing and tripping along with the other teacher at the head with Lila bringing up the rear.

They were going down the street towards the bunch of shadeless eucalyptus trees on the riverbanks of Jasool on a class picnic. It was still early morning but the day was already stoking up and there was very little traffic on the street; milkmen on cycles returning from their rounds, a mendicant, some early risers and constitutionalists and other schoolchildren on their way to class casting envious glances. Ishan had arrived late the night before. He had stepped out early in the morning, as was his practice, to see if his arrival had in any way been anticipated; he wanted to check for any sign of recognition or suspicion.

But he was not remarked upon except for the curious glances bestowed on a stranger, which is only natural in a small town. Ishan could see all too clearly what would happen here with the closure of the mills. Even the narrow-gauge rail track to this dead-end would be overgrown with grasses and the stationmaster himself would be transferred out of this ghost town with its two derelict mills standing guard over their own misbegotten waste. Only the single cinema-house would be full—clogged with a people hungry for the solace of illusion.

Ishan was standing under the shadow of the bridge when he first saw Lila and the others coming towards him skipping and laughing. Lila saw him only when she had almost come up to him. Lila saw him at first as an approaching stranger wobbling in the heat haze. Only slowly did Ishan gain definition in her eyes, like some figure in a photograph undulating and developing in a tray of fluid in the red light of the darkroom. Laughing with instant recognition, she ran up to him.

Seeing his awkwardness, she left him briefly, to confer with the other teacher. Some of the older girls at the back turned towards him and whispered among themselves. Lila returned to him and, the other teacher casting a look in his direction, ordered the last of the straggling gigglers to keep a sharp lookout and not dawdle. At this all the girls turned back to look at Ishan and Lila, except the tail-enders who pushed on ahead.

Ishan and Lila walked away towards the mills and the cemetery at the other end of town, beyond the bend in the river Jasool. She could hardly speak for the suppressed happiness welling up in her. She was suffused with joy.

They turned down a backstreet where the backs of all the houses were already displaying the day's washing hung out to dry. They had been walking without holding hands, without words. As they mounted the stone steps that led to the main street above, Ishan asked Lila about her grandmother, the terror.

When they were all in school together, Lila, her sister, and her two brothers stayed with their grandmother; their parents, who were both engineers, lived in South Africa, where all four children had been born. They were always talking about their grandmother when they were in school because the old woman used to beat them and punish them endlessly at home.

Lila was two years junior to Ishan and Zarina (she had the saddest eyes he had ever seen) was two years his senior; Zarina, as Ishan remembered her, seemed an accident-prone girl: she was always bruised, bandaged or limping; Ashraf was in Ishan's class and Jamil was four years younger than him. Lila said that her grandmother had died only two years ago; Ashraf (bespectacled and timid) studied medicine and returned home to practise in South Africa. Jamil, who was even in those days a sunny sportsman with an open face, ran away from home, was later received into the Roman Catholic church and began working for the St. Vincent de Paul's Society before being ordained a priest here in India. Zarina committed suicide by jumping into a disused well in Govandi.

'My parents wanted me to return to South Africa but I refused to return. When grandmother died, my parents insisted that I return, but by then things were too far gone for words to mean anything really. Even these very words. I wrote to them saying that for me South Africa was only another country and that they would never see me again. I have never written again. They do not even know I am in this town. They should never have made us come away and stay with grandmother in the first place,' she cried. 'They should never have done that, never—poor Zarina. Oh, Zarina! Zarina!' she sobbed. Ishan was equally divided between comforting her and not intruding on her grief. But just as suddenly she collected herself and looked at him. 'And you, what are you doing here? Are you married? Tell me.' Mastering her tears she said again, 'Tell me about yourself. Twenty years! My god!'

Ishan told her that soon after graduation, his parents had arranged his marriage with a girl of their own caste; Ishan had two children and now lived in Delhi in a larger house than the tiny flat he had grown up in. Already they were past the cemetery and found themselves walking across the dry riverbed. On one side were the high walls of the mill topped with broken glass and on the other, where they stood, a row of godowns and warehouses. At this time of the year, and this year particularly, the river Jasool was a malodorous series of puddles fed by the township's gutters. Here and there, in the hollows of dirty water in the dusty riverbed, flyblown buffaloes and pigs were soaking themselves. Lila wiped her eyes and said she really must return to her duties.

Suddenly, out of nowhere, a group of about fifteen or twenty men, mill workers, appeared around them from all sides—some stepping through the filthy water and coming at them across the river. They were converging on Ishan and Lila.

So Ishan's coming here was not a secret after all. They had known it all along and prepared for it in advance. Ishan looked around. There was fear in Lila's dilated eyes brimming with tears again. The mill workers advanced towards them slowly. No one spoke a word. But how had they known Ishan would be here? As they stood around in a silent and menacing circle, three or four people stepped forward and started beating Ishan systematically. The sun broke up into bits in Ishan's eyes. Someone held Lila back. They beat Ishan till he passed out. His perplexities fell from him and he floated out on a sea of pure pain.

Ishan woke up in bed in a strange room, patched and bandaged, aching in every joint. He could not see or speak very well for both his eyes were swollen and he had lost two teeth. He was alone. His ribcage was bandaged with an itchy adhesive tape and he felt a sharp stab of pain with each breath he drew. On the bedside table stood a stack of school copybooks. In his own blurred way, Ishan immediately took in the signs that told him that he was in Lila's place. The window behind the bed opened out onto an enclosed courtyard that was common to the houses built around it; some women were collecting water at the common tap in the centre. When Ishan looked out of the window from his bed, he saw framed in it the face of an old man supporting himself on a stick and two children staring back at him.

The fact that Ishan was up and looking out was obviously a signal for several other faces to appear at the window: among others, two women who wiped their hands on their saris in complete synchronization. The sounds of their whispering were carried to him in a distorted buzzing in his ears. Ishan turned, slid deeper into the bed, and closed his eyes. Sleep. He promptly returned to dreaming of his school days.

In the evening Ishan was woken up by other voices in the hall. He tried to sit up. Lila, a doctor and one of the mill managers came into the room. They discussed Ishan as though he was not present or he was dead. Ishan's days and nights ran into each other. The windows were heavily curtained and the night light in the room burned all the time. He felt much better though he was continuously sedated. This isolation was intermittently broken by the doctors, Lila, representatives from headquarters and the local mill executives. The whole question of the present operation was shelved. Ishan had been granted special leave and recalled to Delhi.

Ishan moved out to the N.K. Lodging House as soon as he was able to. He could return to Delhi whenever he felt up to it. His job here was over. The word from Delhi was that they had indefinitely postponed taking any decision on the Jasool mills. Ishan waited for Lila who was supposed to come and see him at 4.30; but as she was not there until 6 o'clock, Ishan decided to go over to her place. It was not a time of the year for rains and inky dark clouds were drifting up from the south-west. Ishan progressed slowly towards her house. It was not that he was in any pain; all the drugs and his enforced rest had made him quite light-headed. Ishan was actually frightened he might just float away.

People walking past him, the houses, the whole scene of which Ishan was a part, seemed part of another, enchanted world. The streetlights, which just came on, were cancelled out by the failing twilight, increasing the eerie feeling of unreality. The air was getting stuffy under a lowering sky. At the same time, Ishan was aware of a thrilling sensation as though he was reborn. As he turned the corner, Lila rushed past him from behind without noticing him. Ishan called to her. The relief on her face was unmistakable. She had been delayed in school because of an accident involving a child; she had rushed directly from the school to the lodging house only to find Ishan gone and had rushed back, running part of the way, she said, to be in time to receive him. Her eyes sparkled with excitement as though the negative ions in the atmosphere were getting to her.

When they had settled down and she had got her breath back, she told him about Zarina's death. But Ishan wanted to hear nothing of all that. He was sweating with the effort of walking and the sultriness of the unseasonal downpour that threatened to come down any moment. More than anything else, he wanted to lay his head on Lila's breast. He wanted her to cradle him in her lap. He wanted them to return to their childhood, to that secret body of still, sweet water in the hills like a benediction under a palpitating sky when they first got to know each other.

'Zarina committed suicide,' said Lila. 'But we had killed her long before she died.' To keep from sobbing she spoke slowly, every now and then her frame shaken by a periodic shudder from the strain of going on with what she wanted to say, 'You see, my grandmother hated her the most and as for Zarina, she seemed to welcome suffering. I suspect there is something twisted in every saint. We didn't quite see it then but slowly, by degrees, slowly over the years we collaborated with our grandmother against Zarina, beginning with silent non-interference leading to an active participation in physically hurting her, and we ended up by being far worse to Zarina than our grandmother ever was to her or to any of us.' The tears ran down her cheeks and she made no effort to clean herself up. It was as if Lila's words had to come out now or never. 'Did we do what we did as a way of avoiding our grandmother's beatings from being directed at us? What did we ever hope to achieve? Only Jamil did not pass beyond the stage of silent acquiescence. He would run away and hide somewhere when one of us took a swipe at Zarina. Zarina never, never retaliated, never even defended herself. Why, oh God? Why?' Lila folded up, racked by a series of shuddering sobs. Ishan's marriage itself seemed to dissolve in her tears as he gazed at the loosened knot of fine black hair cascading around her face. It started raining outside and that made a sudden difference to the light in the corners of the room. That change in the light or something else made Lila get up, put on the house lights and disappear into the bathroom to put her face to rights. The first thing she said on her return was, 'You said you'd take me to a movie. You promised.' By the time they stepped out after dinner, it had stopped raining and the roads were shining wet under the street lamps. However, the air was steamy and still heavy with the threat of yet more rain. Lila took his hand in her own and threaded fingers with him. At the cinema-house she forgot even herself, totally absorbed in the flickering story on the screen. After the movie she said, 'You don't know how I need the movies. To switch off, forget myself, become whole again, however temporarily. You just don't know.'

Returning home, they were caught in another cloudburst. They ran into a crowd of late-night spectators gathered around a house on fire, hissing and steaming in the downpour. Drenched and laughing they returned home. She was infinitely tender with him as though she would delicately heal once and for all the complex of wounds that time inflicts on the human body with the fragile balm of her feminity. It was pouring outside. To Ishan this was another world where, to complete the illusion, he felt he had found his true being.

He did not want to sleep, he did not want the night to end, and he did not want to wake up to another day with its old-world responsibilities. He could see only too well that the road he was embarked on would be the death of Lila. But he did not or could not turn back or away. It was too late.

Everything seemed different as though he had awoken from the dead. Obviously, this encounter with Lila seemed to have such far-reaching consequences that the world as they knew it earlier was imploding in their embrace. For one of them, at least, things would never be the same again. The next day Ishan wired his office that he was on his way and set out for home, bewildered and light-headed. He knew he would never see Lila again; the more she was touched by their encounter the more she was likely to finish herself off. If his experience of water with Lila in the hills of their childhood was real, was their second coming together a dream? If their second encounter was true, how could that distant first meeting have been false? History, which never repeats itself, sometimes mimics itself. The racing sky outside the train window was overcast. He had encompassed Lila's end as surely as she had helped in the torture of Zarina. That was the only point of lucidity in a world where everything else was suddenly rendered wet and uncertain. When the train stopped at the Manmad junction, he woke up. It was raining heavily now. He immediately entered into the rhythm of the train and dozed off into the new world he'd been given a glimpse of—a world that came into being when he fell asleep and vanished when he woke up. It was late at night when he arrived home.

The light was on in the children's bedroom. Jyotsna opened the door to him and smiling sleepily, whispered, 'Karan has fever.' Obviously, she had dozed off in the chair beside Karan's bed. Swati, the older girl, was asleep in their bed in the other room. Ishan carried Swati back to her own bed, next to Karan's, put out the lights in their room and returned to Jyotsna who was now wide-awake. 'I missed you,' said Jyotsna. Really, nothing had changed. He had needlessly been apprehensive. He had merely to turn away from his allopatric folly. 'Me too,' lied Ishan, willing himself to mean the words that preceded the thought: 'I missed you too.'

A Hangman's Tale

Lok Dutt Tokas was the hangman in the city's central jail. When Tokas was made hangman, it was still a prestigious post. But of late, there had been a falling off in its popularity, with the employees opting for transfers to more profitable positions. Even the number of hangings had come down.

In the good old days, a hanging was a public event, a joyous festival. The announcement was made, well in advance, weeks before the scaffolding was assembled in one of the city's major market squares.

The celebrations went on for weeks and culminated in the main event, which was the hanging. The lights burned late into the night and early morning, and troupes of tumblers, jugglers, dancers and street thespians wove their way through the groggy throng entertaining and shouting imprecations at the passers-by. There were motorcyclists in the well-of-death, dressed in their colourful satin regalia with their leather helmets, goggles and knee-length boots; magicians squatting on reed mats with caged birds that told your fortune by choosing one of several alternative futures uniquely penned and waiting solely for you. There were tattooists and body-painters; self-flagellants clutching bloody whips and lashing themselves as they moved in a circle, bleeding into the sand; spirit possession as a spectator sport in a closed tent with admission tickets. Very large bottles of formalin with the corpses of freaks and malformed creatures—fetuses of creatures that were half-snake, half-man; half-cat, half-human; half-parrot, half-human; a bearded dwarf with gigantic genitals twice his size; and a three-headed man with the body of a buffalo—stood on display. There were masseurs, ear-cleaners, aphrodisiac vendors and so on. After dark, the insomniacs hit the streets: painted women, child-prostitutes, hermaphrodites, and people on the lookout for them. Oh, those were the times! The hangman then was a considerable figure—a personage to be reckoned with—the man at the centre of the festivities.

In spite of the fact that hangings were public events (the municipal authorities declared them holidays), fantastic rumours circulated in whispers about such events. Men, at the moment of hanging, it was said, had erections that would never die down; the body hair and nails of the hanged, in a keratin conspiracy, continued to grow long after death. Every part of the hanged man had a specific use in black magic and the tantric arts; certain secret societies, whose names may not be mentioned, maintained that certain rigorously conducted rituals with a hanged corpse could confer dark powers over others and even raise the dead to life.

Nowadays, even the judges rarely handed down a decent death sentence—something one could recount to the younger generation or point to as an example. There was a lot of nonsense talked about humane, correctional punishment, and the guilty were unceremoniously lynched in secret like criminals in the ancient prison's central courtyard, screened from the eyes of even the convicts, as if the whole thing was an obscene act, something to be ashamed of.

These were some of the unmistakable signs of the times and Tokas read them correctly. He changed with the times, resigned himself to the inevitable, accepting what he could not change but his heart slowed down and he felt a growing emptiness within himself that just refused to be assuaged. In order to break the cycle of boredom and depression he increasingly spent his nights roaming the red-light district and other such places looking for diversions. The clouds refused to lift, wrapping him in a miasma of hopelessness. But, luckily for him, he was saved from these diminished and reduced circumstances by his encounter with Chandralekha, a wet nurse by day and a prostitute by night. Lekha had lost her child in stillbirth two years ago. She succumbed to the solace offered by the folly of a surrogate motherhood. She became a wet nurse—it helped supplement her meagre income and made up, somewhat, for the loss of clientele among the men who found themselves uncomfortable with a lactating woman heaving in their arms.

When Lekha worked as a wet nurse, she was generally inducted into the household under the guise of an ayah or a babysitter. Some households were very particular that she bathe before feeding the baby; they saw to it that she was well fed when nursing. Neglect and discord promptly made their appearance when the infant was weaned away from the breast to processed food formulas. While being a wet nurse was in no way a substitute for the real thing, it had its consolations. They were periods of restful ease when she found she was able to forget herself as she sat cross-legged on the floor with the infant gently jouncing in her lap, holding fast to her index finger and sucking at her nipple. At such moments she wallowed in a glow of well-being. Her cares fell away from her, and she would break into some popular film song, crooning under her breath to the slurping bundle of borrowed joy at her breast. (Once she even nursed two infants simultaneously for a couple whose ten barren years of marriage culminated in twin boys.)

Lekha, at twenty-nine years of age, was a mere slip of a girl. She had straight, black hair, a bronze-brown complexion and a smile that lit up her eyes before reaching her mouth. Each of her features was nondescript; and it was not as if the sum of them, taken together, had any knock down, carrying impact. Yet men who spent time with her found her not just engaging but attractive. She grew on them. The thing that drove some of her admirers away was her conversation which was limited to an endless litany of complaints. She was always whingeing about something or the other. Often, while talking or listening (more the former) she had a way of directing her gaze away, in mid-sentence, with downcast eyes that hinted at an innate and becoming shyness; there was a breathless break in her speech, which, while not exactly calculated to reinforce belief in her complaints, engendered a certain protectiveness towards her, in the listener, nonetheless. She was a runaway from an orphanage and had begun life as a bar dancer before she began dispensing her favours to the more generous of her admirers. Even as an adult, she continued playing a game with herself that was a carry over from her childhood. This consisted of identifying strangely nondescript places, which one could enter and become invisible—areas before one's very eyes that one never noticed. The more public and secret, the better: a broken wall beside a blighted pomegranate tree on a disused traffic island in an old quarter of the town; a much frequented pedestrian footbridge; a collapsed tin hoarding on the thorny verge of the main highway. She saw herself in such places looking out at acquaintances who blindly passed her by.

When her pregnancy ended in the stillbirth of a girl child (whom she had dreamed of naming Dia-Lata), she made up her mind that she must have a daughter. The doctors made it clear to her that because of certain complications, she could never carry another child for the full term of the pregnancy. Most of her dreams centred on her mothering a laughing girl playing hopscotch in the dust with the other kids.

No orphanage or donor agency would consider a request for adoption from a person in her circumstances, and she knew it. Her earlier notion that she must have a daughter now became an unshakeable conviction.

When Tokas first met Lekha, it was one of those smoky winter nights with the open drains steaming on the ill-lit roadside. It was past midnight and Tokas was making his way rather aimlessly through the thinning crowds, bored out of his mind, when he happened on Lekha. He was momentarily drawn to the novelty of her chatter for he was accustomed only to the ritualistic silence common on such occasions. Lekha talked about her problems with an unselfconsciousness that was unique. It introduced an element of togetherness that Tokas found exciting beyond anything that sex had earlier provided. As he smoked beedi after beedi and listened to Lekha, he found himself attracted to the intimacy of her revelations. In her room, she confessed that she was lactating, that she worked as a wet-nurse during the day, that she had lost her child sometime ago. For her part, Lekha found it strange that a man should pay her and not paw her; instead, he sat smoking at the foot of the bed listening intently to the story of her life, which was nothing but a list of troubles she never grew tired of recounting, with new embellishments in each retelling.

She told him that the doctors had told her she could never have a child, but she was determined she said to have a daughter whom she would nurture with love and care and send out into the world to lead a life of ease and happiness that was never her lot. Would he help her? No one had ever asked him for such a thing. He jumped at the chance to be of help to her. She quickly glossed over his agreement to help her by making it clear to him that nothing in their personal lives would change.

'We are not getting, like, married to each other or anything. So don't get any funny ideas. Nor will you be, like, a father or anything.'

Tokas agreed to these conditions readily enough. For him, it was as though the whole of his life until then had been a mere dry run. But that was not enough for her. 'It'll be, like quite tough,' she said. 'It won't be easy or anything because we have to be patient and, like, on the lookout constantly. We have to cultivate like the nurses and ward boys in the maternity hospitals. Pay them to keep their eyes and ears open.' Whatever the exact import of her words, for him they were couched in the argot of hope.

Tokas loved her manner of using words like like and anything. He agreed they would have to be careful. 'The orphanages and adoption agencies are of no use to people like us. But there are lost children, homeless street children and runaways. We have to look for your daughter among such castaways.'

Hearing these words Lekha suddenly realized that her vague longings were at last taking real shape. She grabbed Tokas's hand and pressed it rhythmically against her breast, kneading it as if to give form to her dreams, until her blouse and bra were wet with her expressed milk. 'See?' she asked, and when Tokas peered at her cleavage, she pulled his head down on to her breasts. With a single, deft movement Tokas tore open the eyes and hooks of her blouse. Most of the women he had been with wore blouses with press-buttons. The grey light of early morning seeped in through the louvred, wooden slats of the window and the shuttered ventilator above. It had been a new kind of night for both of them.

Tokas was fascinated with Lekha. She represented for him the small sum of everything he had wanted in life but had never thought he would have. For Lekha, he was just another sap. She regarded him with the tolerance reserved for all her visitors. True, he was a kindly hulk who loved listening to her grumble but she found him quite wonky in his own way. For instance, he would pay her for the night and not do anything to her; sometimes he would wait outside while she received other paying men on his paid-up time. These things did not really matter to Lekha and naturally, she thought they didn't matter to Tokas either. In his own way Tokas really loved Lekha. He knew that he was not anything special in her scheme of things but all the same, he seemed to welcome the fact that, over time, she slowly invaded and took possession of his whole being. Whether he was with her or away from her, she shaped his days and gave structure to his nights. Lekha was more than just home to him in ways he did not understand.

Mantara's father was a moribund, alcoholic widower whose disintegrating shack in the slum was far more stable than the owner who was coming apart on a daily if not hourly basis. Mantara was a bruised and abandoned child—a needy child with dreamy eyes in a starved gymnast's body. She had an inborn ability to twist and fold herself in amazing ways that made the other street children gasp with astonishment. It also meant that, unlike the other girls, she was the target of bullies. When Tokas first spotted her, Mantara had a bandage on her forehead, stained with gentian violet that held down her twin pigtails plaited with red ribbons. The next day, Tokas stood next to Lekha at the top of the stone stairway connecting the streets on two levels and pointed to some ragged children at play on the curbside below. The bandage had come off and Mantara, who was wearing a blue-green kurta (far too large for her) as a frock, had tied herself into a knot on the pavement in the centre of a circle of urchins yelling appreciatively.

Tokas threw a scare into the girl's sodden father and gave him some booze and money. The girl had to be slowly won over with blandishments. She played along and even accepted the new life, calling Lekha, Amma—but she just refused to be renamed Dia-Lata. She chose to stick to her old name: Mantara. She was muckle-mouthed (with a magic smile) and had long eyelashes that cast their shadows on her dusky cheeks. She too smiled with her great, big eyes; that and the lisp in Mantara's voice convinced Lekha that the two of them had been made for each other. After the arrival of Mantara, Lekha took great care to meet her clients outside the house. She stopped visitors from coming to the house on business. She did not want Mantara's future to be a replay of her own past. This increased her price and even her work as a wet-nurse tapered off; this was partly because of the hair follicles in her left armpit showing a tendency to become infected. This was the dark prelude to the cancer in her left breast, which would slowly mature and reach its full flowering much later bearing the fruit that is common to all such growths.

Lekha's new life centred on Mantara. For her, Tokas was a useful man to have around, someone who heard her out with the kind of patience she had never encountered before. However, the minute attention she paid to Mantara left her very little time to think about herself to say nothing of Tokas. Tokas's world was Lekha. Mantara appeared in the corner of his eye only in so far as she was the focus of Lekha's maternal possessiveness. For Lekha, Mantara represented the redressal of the balance for the squalour and travails of a hitherto kinless life.

One August afternoon, Lekha sat on the edge of her bed and watched Mantara's sleeping form in her own bed across the room divided by a bedsheet-curtain. A flute was producing some really sweet notes somewhere across the street, and a shaft of sunlight from the unshuttered ventilator high above fell like grace on the young girl's sleeping form below. Lekha went up to Mantara and touched the girls' forehead to check her temperature. Mantara was just recovering from a bout of influenza. Just then, she awoke and sat up in bed and stretched herself with a slow, luxurious and sensual motion, her raven black hair back lit by the afternoon sun. Lekha's eyes roved over the other's lithe body in an infinitely gentle caress as though she feared she would generate some static in the loose contact between them causing Mantara to suffer an electrical burn. All at once, Lekha realized that her daughter was no more a girl but a beautiful young woman. Just then, Mantara turned towards her and smiled, while running her fingers through her hair. Time to get her married off, thought Lekha, an automatic smile masking her abstracted gaze as with her right hand she felt the tiny bead growing in her left breast.

The tests revealed a growth and the biopsy indicated that it was a malignant form of cancer—a mastectomy was indicated. However, Lekha refused point blank to go under the knife. She was more than willing to take her chances with the disease. Tokas suggested to Lekha that they make a pilgrimage to the shrine in Nashik. On behalf of the whole family, Tokas fasted for two days, prayed and gave alms to the poor preparatory to the journey. In spite of the sombre reason for their outing, it had its holiday-happy moments for the threesome.

All temple-towns are the same and no two temple-towns are ever alike! At the railway junction where one has to change from the broad-gauge to the meter-gauge lines, there were devotees and pilgrims talking about the sanctity of such a journey—how Nashik was the most powerful place on earth, how magnets failed to work there and how clocks and watches ran backwards if they ran at all. It was said that the energy vibrations in Nashik were so potent that they effected cures even in chronic unbelievers.

The train emerged through a dust storm that was darker

than the tunnel it had passed through earlier, and came into Nashik in the early afternoon sun. The place was like any month in an Indian calendar with its screaming colours and gaudy gods. The platform was swarming with cripples, some of whom were beggars, while the others were genuinely handicapped believers seeking a cure. Lekha held on to Mantara's hand to prevent her getting lost in the crowd. She need not have worried with Tokas keeping a protective eye on both of them. Both sides of the three streets that converged on the railway station were clogged with pilgrim-special buses and cycle rickshaws plastered with garish cinema posters. These buses plied on no fixed routes and were amenable to any suggestions as to destination, their only advertisement being the name of the latest movie showing on their colour television, complete with surround-sound. Mantara wanted an orange soda so the three of them ended up downing bottles of the fizzy drink that had been chilling in a rusting icebox. They slept as the bus sped through the town past innumerable temples along the sacred river, towards the particular shrine of their choice.

The stench of sweat, crushed flowers and burnt oil wafted in the air as the crowds pressed towards the large cave opening in the tiny hillock past the granite trelliswork adorned with millions of knotted threads—the traditional votive offerings to the gods. At last, it was all done: the thread tying, the prayers, the mumbled vows before the invisible deity in the inner darkness of the sanctum sanctorum, surrounded by the bare-torsoed priests chanting Sanskrit hymns.

That night in the dak bunglow, the disease presented its first, deadly warning. When the night watchman was calling the second hour of the morning, they were woken up to

Lekha vomiting blood in retching spasms. Thinking she was dying, Lekha who had, on the whole, been indifferent to Tokas, now pulled him to herself and made him promise her in a hoarse whisper that he would look after and care for Mantara after she was dead and gone. Their return home was instantaneous as in a dream. Lekha slept through the journey, which seemed to last no longer than the blink of an eye.

At home, Lekha got worse day by day. She was nauseous and could not eat anything. She grew weak and wasted while first her left breast and then her right breast began swelling. The left breast was swollen far more than the right one, giving her a lopsided look as she lay in bed casting her mind back to her earliest memories.

She replayed her stark childhood images stripped of nostalgia and unadorned by anything like happiness: There was her mother in their one-room house, talking to a hairy visitor with spectacles while she lay hidden under some burlap sacks under the common staircase to the building. There was the rumble of distant thunder and the occasional flash of lightning. She could not see them but she could hear the stranger's voice and her mother's unfamiliar laughter. She could see the rain pelting the cast iron fence outside the areaway littered with vegetable peels; and beyond that, a donkey unmindful of the downpour, rubbing its itchy back against the railings. Under cover of the gunny bags Lekha hugged her imaginary brother, Munna, to herself and talked to him in whispers: 'We'll go away together. We'll go far, far away somewhere where, like, no one can ever find us. There we'll play like anything in the rain. What fun it'll be to roll about in the slush . . .' One summer afternoon Lekha had decided that Munna was ill and hungry; she was in the middle of feeding him when her mother turned her out of the room because of the two visitors who had come calling—strong, young men with loud voices. Lekha fell asleep under the tamarind tree and when she returned home, she found her mother crouching on the floor, cradling a broken finger in her left hand, head bent down with tears in her eyes. 'What happened?' Lekha asked and her mother, with averted face trying to hide a purpling bruise on her temple, said, 'What happened! What happened! I broke my finger, that's what happened. Now get out of the house and let me get on with my work.'

It had been a hard life but it was not without its rare moments of joy. In her fevered delirium Lekha spoke of these dreams of her lost childhood in disconnected whispers with such ease that one would have thought such gibberish was the common parlance of her daily life. The approaching end had transfigured Lekha into a starving, saint-like figure whose bones burned brightly through her transparent skin. Tokas came whenever he could make it. He was full of augurous concern; he held Lekha's bony hand in his own massive, gnarled hands hoping to comfort her. She was generally oblivious of her surroundings, breaking into reality now and then with her calls to Mantara. She had no word for Tokas—not that he expected anything: he was content to be there for her if she ever needed anything. When Mantara did speak to her, she was unable to get through to her most of the time.

With Lekha's death, Tokas was lost. He was unravelling, but slowly. Over time he was going to pieces in bits and parts; the incidents were so varied, and separated in time and place, that an accurate reading of them as progressive events distancing him from reality was nearly impossible. In any case, it was something no one else knew anything about.

The first time it happened, he was sitting in a local railway bogey when the general hubbub gave way to total silence; the talkative mob around him continued mouthing whatever it was that each was saying but no words issued forth. Welling up from this deep well of silence, Tokas heard Lekha's voice repeating the last words of the last hanged man to Tokas at the gallows. Then the chatter and noise in the railway compartment resumed its former decibel level. He looked around, turning his head this way and that: nobody else had heard anything.

He was sitting in the prison office, working on some files when he blacked out. It was pouring outside. He came to in the corner of the crematorium reserved for the nameless and unclaimed corpses waiting in line for their funeral pyres to be lit. On the other side, other pyres were burning. He was dust dry under the tarpaulin while the dead lay soaking in the dripping landscape waiting for the long wait to be over. The place was familiar to him for he had been there before to cremate the disowned bodies of hanged men. His vacant gaze settled on the banked embers of the funeral pyre by his side. There, in the dying fire, he saw Lekha's undying eyes looking at him through the falling rain. Before he could react, the burning figure held out its melting arm to him in a piteously pathetic gesture before dissolving and subsiding into a glowing heap that sent up a spray of sparks.

The third, secret incident happened that summer. It was a slow Sunday morning and Tokas was taking his ease at home. He could hear the children at play outside in the blinding glare. Mantara, who did not care to join in their games, was in the kitchen pretending to be a grown-up. Tokas was sitting on the cement floor under the whirling ceiling fan trying to organize the day's newspaper by aligning its corners and folds when an unbelievable thing happened. He could not find his right arm. He could not see it or even feel it with his other hand. He rushed to the mirror. There he saw an image not of himself but of Lekha, with the missing limb. He was immobilized with fear and humiliation. He collapsed in a heap under the mirror hanging from a nail in the wall. He was sopping wet with perspiration before he hit the floor, with his eyes shut tight. When he woke up it was night and he had only a vague and inexact memory of the event that had put him to sleep under the mirror from behind which the house lizard was calling. It did not seem to matter then, because he was whole and intact.

It was spring weather in the middle of winter when Tokas woke up from a dream of Lekha, in the middle of the night, to find that he was lactating. He threw off his bedclothes and tore open his kurta in panic. There was milk oozing from his hairy dugs; there was a slight itchiness around the nipples where the old seepage had dried into powder. He rushed to Mantara and putting his arms under her sleeping form, he lifted the startled girl on to his cross-legged lap and pressed her protesting face to his chest. Mantara, screaming and crying, broke free from him and pressed herself into a corner of the room facing Tokas, her hands clamped to her mouth in horror, as he, bare-chested and in pyjamas, stumbled out into the chilly night.

Tokas disappeared that night. The days lengthened like shadows into months and the months into seasons. Mantara changed her name to Dia-Lata. She, who had against all odds come in off the streets, now found herself once again a part of the same old traffic. Earlier, her young age on the street had conferred on her a certain kind of pedestrian safety in numbers, which was now withdrawn. But the shutting of this door opened the way to the dance bars and security of a different kind. It was Dia-Lata's first step on the stairway to the stars.

In the world of the dance bars, one might have thought that a young thing like Dia-Lata would have a longish waiting period. Providentially, quite the opposite was true in her case. Dia-Lata was a spectacular success from day one. The word on the street was that the sensational dancing contortionist was a virgin. The fact was that the owner of the dance bar who was responsible for her safety and success had extracted his price before introducing her to the swarming eyes and grasping hands of the paying public in his establishment. Dia-Lata returned to the ways of her adoptive mother whose appeased ghost presumably joined in the applause that brought her nightly routine to a close. Her name soon became a household word and pictures of her iconic face graced public spaces. Dia-Lata enjoyed star status even before she entered the movies and made the silver screen her own. She adorned the covers of glossy magazines. So popular was she that pictures of her were edging out the usual depictions of gods and their consorts on calendars and almanacs. Later ages would see Dia-Lata's face as a sign of the times.

Tokas returned to the city without any inkling that he had returned to the city. He was exhausted and driven wild by his years of fruitless search. He came very early in the morning, under cover of darkness. It was the foggiest winter in recorded history and Tokas wore himself out trudging the streets—as in all the other cities—looking for the likeness of Lekha in the ghostly figures huddled on the roadside in the murky lamplight. The invisible crows around the crumbling prison towers could be heard a long way off in the heavy dawn mist, which clung like tattered pennants to the granite ramparts. In that poor light one would have had to come up really close to just about make out the hairy, naked form of Tokas hanging from a noose of his own making from the scaffolding in the jail's central courtyard.

Just before 9/11

He changed slowly after he met Mansur Ali Roedad. Even the late budding of his relationship with Rachel Stansted could not bring him back. In the end he became what he was.

Ehtesham did not leave behind any taped martyrdom testimony or goodbye letters to anyone. What he did leave behind him though, apart from a few meagre personal effects, were the glimmerings of a private diary (with a single entry: preachy rather than personal) that ended before it barely began; and a folder filled with A4 size papers.

Seventy-eight of these loose sheets of paper were found filled with repetitive accounts of corpses being found in lush surroundings with minor alterations and extensive additional notes on nature cribbed from Rachel's work. The subtle atrocity in these failed attempts at writing is not immediately apparent; only history makes the horror slowly available to us in time. All the writings, in Ehtesham's hand, were interlaced with doodles and scribbles. These papers were taken into a single file, termed 'The Notes', for inclusion into the growing body of evidence. After the carnage of 9/11 one of the trails led the investigators, via the flying school in Daytona Beach, to a small town in North Dakota. 'The Notes' presented the only hint on the missing Rachel Stansted. On the strength of this slender lead, several water bodies that Rachel and Ehtesham most probably visited were dragged in, but to no avail. Of the wretched descriptions of the seven bodies found—all blonde teenaged runaways—here are two samples:

> The first body to be found was in the Bayou country with katydids hovering over the canebrakes. The body of the teenaged runaway girl had been in the water for an unknown length of time providing sustenance to bowfins and salamanders. Disfigured and disintegrating, the corpse with long, trailing yolk-blonde hair was held fast in the tangle of the root system of the giant cypress, swaying and drifting several levels beneath the wobbling scum. The water was cola coloured and the shuttered, green half-light was gloomy. The visibility was very poor, and blobs of dappled light amid the floating leaf litter only added to the confusion.
>
> The second body was found in Missouri—she was a leggy, nineteen-year-old blonde. It looked as though she had been killed and dropped into autumn somewhere between the Osage Plains and the Ozark Hills. Autumn is a dye that seeps down south from northern Missouri in mid-September, reaching its richest display in the third week of October. She must have been killed well before that. Then the burning colours fade, the leaves dry out, curl and

> begin to fall, carpeting the earth in coral and terracotta shades. Swarms of migrating monarch butterflies feed on the poisonous milkweed shrubs and the wild yellow lilies that trail along the ground. Towards the end of November, wild turkeys scratching the ground in search of acorns under the quilt of fallen leaves had uncovered the body of the girl decaying under the slow yellows of the sweet gum and the late crimson berries of the possum haw.

Abu Bakar Ehtesham was slight of build with clear, sharp features. He wore his black, slightly wiry hair combed back. The eagerness apparent in his fresh face was offset by the opacity of an innate reserve compounded by shyness; a hint of this rectitude was reflected in the veiled attitude his hooded eyes assumed in moments of intense passion: a drowning, inward look that was blind to the outside world. It was a face that would age badly but in his case it would never come to that.

He was not particularly religious in his outlook though he came from an orthodox family which had lived for generations in the Allama-Iqbal Chowk area of Sialkot. He did not pray five times a day or wear a beard with a clean-shaven upper lip. He was an engineer who had lost interest in engineering; he took up nature studies in graduate school in Moffit, North Dakota. He felt himself strangely drawn to the badlands and ghost towns in the region. The morbid inhospitality of such places excited his affections. He craved the obscurity of a small town and Moffit seemed just the right place in which to lose himself and pursue his anonymous destiny. But after graduation, he opted out of things generally, listening to those stations that still beamed folk protest music on his cracked car radio, drifting from one part-time job to another. He could not bring himself to return home or face his people cloaked in the garb of failure. Without knowing it, he was desperately searching for himself in the growing gap between his faith and the world as he found it around himself or for something that would bridge the abyss and make him whole by expunging his sense of being incomplete. It did not help to be kinless and alone in a land of shamelessly individualistic loners, particularly when one came from a country whose people were held together between the twin parentheses of kin and community under the protective canopy of religion.

And so he stayed on in America, hitting the road occasionally in his ancient jalopy, growing more and more lonely, earning a precarious living by working on an ad hoc basis with the Fish and Wildlife Services in nature reserves and protected sanctuaries. It was at this very low point in his life that Mansur first contacted him. Mansur approached him in the college cafeteria. He was clutching a copy of *Jonathan Livingston Seagull* and one of Antoine de Saint-Exupery's *The Little Prince*. Mansur was neither a teacher nor a student though he did conduct himself with the natural confidence of a leader if not a teacher; in fact, he was not from Moffit. Why was he here? What did he do for a living? How did he manage to zero in on Ehtesham? These were some of the questions to which Mansur would not provide the answers just yet. He looked boyish but he was much older than he looked; he was totally secretive with a steady patter designed as a perfect blind behind which he hid himself. Mansur made it indirectly clear to Ehtesham at the very outset that their chance coming together was exactly that—entirely accidental. Later, he was expansive, even excited on the subject of flying and the freedom that it bestowed on its practitioners. Such was his infectious enthusiasm that it penetrated even Ehtesham's desultory insularity.

The meeting with Mansur was the defining moment that would give shape to and round off Ehtesham's life. Perhaps it was the instant fellowship of a shared religion, the winsome persuasiveness of Mansur's personality that was deceptively light-hearted and carefree on the surface, his own low ebb or a combination of all these factors. Ehtesham, clutching the two books that had been gifted him, had agreed to visit Mansur in Florida, at the very earliest.

Though not an extravagant person, Mansur was a generous and thoughtful host. It was a fine Friday morning in mid-May as they followed the road from Lake Okeechobee snaking its way past the waves of saw-grass heading towards the mangrove estuaries of the salty gulf. It was the very end of the dry cycle in the alternating climates of the everglades, and Ehtesham was drawn to the ferns, mosses and lichens clustered in the dark shade of the giant cypresses. Later in the afternoon thunderheads darkened the sky, signalling the onset of the spring thunderstorms that marked the beginning of the wet season in that part of the country.

There was a melodramatic sunset followed by early dark. They were towelled dry with steaming mugs of coffee before them. Ehtesham asked Mansur if he would be saying his evening prayers. Mansur said, 'No. You go ahead if you want to. Or would you like to go to the neighbourhood mosque?' Ehtesham carefully considered the matter and said no. At night they watched video clips of bird migrations, flight dynamics and avian aerobatics. Wonderfully fatigued after a day of sightseeing and movie watching, they sprawled about, listening to the rain outside and talked late into the night as sporadic flashes of lightning lit up the windows of the sleep-bound tenement building. There was a sudden cut in the power supply followed by the sound of thunder. Like children in stormy weather they rushed to the windows and saw the city around them plunged into darkness in the pelting rain. During the extended outage what they said to each other was interspersed with long silences as between old friends. Mansur who did most of the talking began with his spiel on flight, and in no time had piloted the conversation gradually but steadily to personal matters. He spoke about his own people with deep dissatisfaction verging on distaste. 'Both my father and brother are wholly complicit in my country's corrupt government which is propped up by America. For all practical purposes my country is engaged in selling its own people in exchange for tainted money under the guise of trade in petroleum. America will go to war with a country in order to make a gift of democracy to it. Yet there is no breath of democracy in the corrupt regimes of even a single one of its Islamic allies. I am telling you but I've never before mentioned this to anyone: some day I'll tell you what my father has done if I can bring myself to narrate it. Oh, the shame of it! People don't know what is really happening in our part of the world. I'll show you the material—the final proof—that friends have sent me. You won't believe it.'

'Show me,' said Ehtesham, sitting up.

'Not now,' said Mansur. 'There is no light and anyway once you see it, you'll never be the same again. Some other time—I promise. After all, I must admit that from the moment

I set eyes on you I knew I was not looking at a pious phoney but a true believer.'

These words set up a vibration in Ehtesham as though half of him was on the point of catching up with his fugitive other half; for an instant, it seemed possible that there was a fit between his beliefs and the reality around him. But the moment passed. 'I want your advice,' said Mansur. 'I have been thinking about it for quite some time now. Should I return home or stay on here in America to make even more money?'

Ehtesham was taken aback with the suddenness and the nature of the question posed. While he struggled to find a suitable answer, Mansur said, 'See, that's what I mean about your honesty. There are so many things I must tell you about. I have so much to say to you and so little time to say it. Don't think about it. Should I stay or go? Just give me your gut response.'

'Stay on in America. Don't go home,' said Ehtesham, without knowing why he said it.

'You are right. How can one return to a country where one's mothers and sisters are dishonoured by foreign infidels?' asked Mansur rhetorically, after a long silence, only to drop the subject as abruptly as he had taken it up. 'My grandfather—he wandered off into the desert one day and never returned. Even stranger was the fact that here was a home-bound man who never ventured out who, just the day before his disappearance, started talking about the desert in the heart of each of us that could be greened only by traversal. Eight months or so later, his part-gnawed and wholly desiccated body was found hundreds of miles away in a dry wadi among the sand dunes by some camel traders. He was brought home and given a proper burial. He was a saint-like person, a Sufi, who never attended the mosque—not even on Fridays. Prayer was part of the circadian rhythm of his life. Every breath he took, sleeping or awake, was a prayer. He once told me, "The Bedouins have a saying: be careful what you desire, for surely it will come true." I told him I desired nothing and he shook his head sadly and said, "You are young. A man will come into your life one day. You cannot seek him out or hasten that day of reckoning. He will find you in good time, and he will show you the way."'

'And did it happen that way?' asked Ehtesham who found himself intimately drawn into the story.

'Yes,' said Mansur. 'But these things are not clear cut. It happens to you and you do not know it. It is so gradual and insidious that a lifetime of faith and waiting is sometimes not enough. What is lucid as light is the end in view. That is what one must never lose sight of. However long the haul, one must stay the course.' He made a gesture with his extended hand and erect, open palm to indicate a straight path and a distant goal, to emphasize his words; it made a misshapen shadow in the flickering candlelight. They fell silent again and watched the dark windowpanes framing the periodic flashes of lightning.

'Cats,' said Mansur. 'I am allergic to them. I suffer from asthma. Once, in a friend's house in Badr-Hunayn, I got an attack. They swore up and down that neither they nor their neighbours had any pets. But a quick search of the garden revealed a feral cat hiding in the tool shed. I use a nasal inhaler whenever I begin sneezing. They say those with allergies live long. But who wants to live long anyway?'

'Yes,' he said bitterly after a long pause. 'Go home and do

what? Better the land of the conqueror than one's own shackled and fettered country, that beloved land of trackless sand criss-crossed by numberless tribes . . . made luminous by the Prophet, peace be upon him . . .' His voice trailed off even as the candle guttered, and on that sleepy note of desperate humiliation a long silence ensued that finally stretched out into sleep.

After a late lie-in on Saturday morning, Ehtesham woke up bleary-eyed with a crick in his neck to find Mansur giving the finishing touches to their lunch. 'Lentils tempered with onions and tomatoes,' announced Mansur with a pinch of pride. 'Fried cauliflower and potato, boiled rice and yogurt with diced cucumber. I learnt cooking from another Pakistani friend.' And there was left-over chicken curry that he did not mention.

That afternoon they drove down to Mansur's Flying Club and Pilot Certification Center in Daytona Beach. The sky was clear, but they double-checked the weather reports to rule out thunderstorms or freakish weather. On a satellite map Mansur pointed out the flight route they would take and the likely places for the best thermals. Even though Mansur had a multi-engine commercial pilot's licence, he took his guest up into the air in an engineless glider, the better to give him a true feel for flying. Ehtesham, who was not afraid of heights, was exhilarated with the rush of air. They returned home in high spirits like schoolboys, with two sky blue t-shirts with the words ALOFT printed in fleecy, white letters, back and front.

Ehtesham first met Rachel along the margins of an alkaline lake, minutely examining some fungal outgrowth among the chaparral. Ehtesham momentarily paused behind the squatting figure with her blonde mane on a nature trail when, sensing his presence (she was suddenly assailed by a strong loamy, woody smell), she volunteered the information that she was working on lichens, without turning to look at him. Ehtesham, who was too shy to have said the first word, allowed a question to escape him before he was even aware of it: 'Are they algae or fungi?'

Rachel turned briefly, with her glowing smile and the searchlight of her baby blue eyes aimed at him, as much as to say she could recognize a true botanist when she saw, or even heard, one before returning her attention to the work at hand. But however little or much her words may have moved him, it was the radiance of her smile that did it for him; that, and her flowing, golden tresses. For Ehtesham, it was his first relationship—however circumstantial, small and inhibited—with a person of the opposite sex who was not related to him; as it was, he had to overcome his vast store of reserve and yes, his repugnance–attraction for women who thought nothing of showing their arms, legs or hair in public. He was of a different persuasion that found aesthetic solace in the veiled face in shadow, in the flash of hands and feet in the sudden glare of sunlight, in the escaped ringlet of hair outside the headscarf and in the hint or suggestion of hidden grace in the folds that draped and softly defined the feminine form.

Rachel was a chubby blonde who had managed to extricate herself from a claustrophobic relationship just after obtaining her doctoral degree when she met up with Ehtesham. They met occasionally, drank coffee together and chatted about impersonal things. If she was in good spirits she thought he gave off a fine smell of wet earth as after a dust-settling, first rain; if she happened to be in a tetchy mood—which was very rare—she thought his body odour was reminiscent of nothing more than a fresh grave. For Ehtesham it was the novelty of the thing. For Rachael it was a welcome break from her introspection which was all too often an exercise in blaming herself for the things she'd done or left undone in her previous relationship with Cody. It was just that Cody Guthrie was not for her. She was quite clear about one thing though: she was not looking for a new relationship just yet. Not after Cody the suffocator. All she wanted for now was to breathe deeply and take it easy. For Rachel the stranger from the opposite part of the world was merely a way of passing the time. Nothing more.

Given these thwarting obstacles on both sides, their conversation had a staccato quality that was limited to their shared interest in the common areas of their work. 'We still do not understand the exact relationship between fungi and algae in lichen,' said Ehtesham. 'Is it symbiotic or parasitic?'

'It is no more difficult to understand than any other relationship,' said Rachel, who had a wry sense of humour.

'And yet they seem to flourish where fungi and algae are rare. Lichens are to be found thriving in sweet and brackish waters, deserts, tropical forests and the freezing tundra. They make their homes on living tortoise shells, the carapace of beetles, rocks, soil, trees, grasslands and sinkholes.'

'In the polar regions', said Rachel, 'lichens have been studied as clocks to establish the lapsed time in the speed of glacial retreat.'

'They may be bitter tasting, yet they form the primarily winter food source of snail, hare and moose.'

'It is used in the manufacture of dyes, perfumes and medicines.'

'In fact, if we didn't have lichens,' said Rachel with a laugh, 'we'd have to invent them.'

This was the unpromising start of their distanced relationship which was itself a kind of long-drawn-out farewell.

Ehtesham and Mansur drove past a mosque. Empty, white clouds raced across the sky, driven by a stiff breeze. Seeing the devout lining up for prayers, Mansur said, 'They are a simple and good people, but we have each of us a different duty to perform. Prayer will not do for all of us. Some prayers, it is true, are answered while others remain unanswered. But our duty is to find answers for which there are no prayers.'

They were in high spirits because Ehtesham, like Mansur before him, had just obtained his commercial pilot's licence. In the last eighteen months Ehtesham's visits to Florida had increased in number and duration. He spent less and less time in North Dakota. On his last visit there he managed to contact Rachel who had just returned from a field trip to Missouri. She showed him her notes and photographs and the two of them discussed the work like old colleagues. They were in such fine accord that Rachel for the first time wondered whether there was something more to the relationship between Ehtesham and herself than either of them suspected. It was just one of those moments that sometimes happened when things are great between two people. Even Ehtesham was moved as never before. True, Rachel's touch had been as light as the bat of an eyelash but he was suffused with a warm sense of well-being; it was not unlike the feeling that flooded him when Mansur hugged him after his maiden solo flight. She gave him her project reports on the managed wilds of the Bayou country and the Ozarks Hills. He promised to go through them and return them to her with his suggestions.

At first Ehtesham thought that Mansur was a loner like himself. But he changed his mind, over time, when he saw how constantly busy Mansur was kept with the telephone calls he received. Once he even broke into Arabic briefly, before reverting to English. Also, Mansur was often out of station, visiting friends, he said. Once, when they were drinking coffee in a shopping mall, Ehtesham saw a bearded young man waving familiarly to Mansur who not only ignored him but changed the angle of his chair to cut off visual contact with him. It was a momentary lapse but Ehtesham caught it, and Mansur who read the signs of what had happened was mildly embarrassed but dismissive of the whole thing. A similar thing had happened when one of the flying instructors mentioned a common friend to Mansur who pretended the name was new to him

Once, Mansur drew his attention to an abandoned, disintegrating factory in the heart of the urban sprawl by pointing to it with his inhaler. Mansur had earlier shown him the sights of the city which included a long and lingering look at a car graveyard. It was then that the half-formed thought flickered through Ehtesham's mind that something in Mansur sought and was deeply satisfied by the feel and sight of rust and twisted metal in the props and furniture surrounding him; he did not recognize then that that dire need in Mansur was but a part of the larger drive in him to general destruction; it was only natural that it did not register with any clarity in Ehtesham given his own subconscious attraction to wasted landscapes like abandoned and deserted townships rotting in the sun.

After a frugal meal at a vegan deli, they ambled down the street taking in the crisp April night air. It was close to midnight and the pedestrian traffic was clotted around street lamps, fire hydrants and neon signs. As they stood chatting by a parking meter, two women appeared out of nowhere and walked past them. One of them brushed Ehtesham's arm and the other broke into giggles. As they moved away, one of them turned back and uttered what sounded like an obscenity when Mansur grabbed his arm and the two of them turned away in unison in a skewed rejection of the incident and the context that made it possible. Mansur was unusually quiet as they made their way home to the rented tenement block and Ehtesham's mind was troubled by images of a naked Rachel look-alike mewling and shimmying in ecstasy under a man who bore an unmistakable resemblance to himself.

That night Mansur asked him if he had a girlfriend. Ehtesham told him he had a friend who was a girl.

'Is she American?'

'Yes,' said Ehtesham, who had earlier mentioned Rachel in passing to Mansur on more than one occasion.

'Good,' said Mansur. 'Tell me about her.'

Ehtesham told him what little he knew about Rachel.

'Can you stop seeing her? I mean, break with her forever?'

'Yes,' said Ehtesham with complete confidence.

'It may not be as easy as you think,' said Mansur. 'Your break with her may come unstuck. She may want to return to you at a later date whatever your feelings for her may be.'

'It is not that kind of a relationship,' said Ehtesham. 'In any case, whatever the nature of the relationship, the break will be final.' Ehtesham, who now understood that this was a test he could not afford to fail, said that he was quite capable of doing whatever was required of him.

The next day Ehtesham returned to Moffit where he still maintained a rented room though he hardly spent any time there at all. He returned to Florida after an extended absence of over three weeks. Rachel went missing and was never heard of again.

When Ehtesham next met Mansur, he told him that Rachel was dead. Mansur looked at him and then looked away; he did not say a word on the subject. What he did say though was: 'You know, I told you about my grandfather who told me a man would come into my life who would show me the way? And you asked me if it had happened to me?'

'Yes,' Ehtesham said, 'and you said these things are not clearly defined.'

'I said that to delay things,' said Mansur. 'The time has now come for you to meet the man who knows the way.'

'For me,' said Ehtesham shyly, 'you are that man.'

Mansur shook his head. 'When you meet my friend, everything will be clear. No conflict, no choice, no confusion. But before the paradise must come the hard work. I promised to show you some films. We'll see the films tonight and tomorrow we meet my friend.'

The single entry in Ehtesham's diary:

> *10th September 2001*
> *My name does not matter because I do not matter. It is only a way of trying to begin. Now that I know I'll never return home, I long for it with an aching need not unlike the one I feel for Rachel. World events have conspired to make America (which I am learning to despise) my final destination, my destiny. I have not met a single American who did not strike me as being a good person. Americans are a lonely people with each one going his or her own way without reference to their families or God. The women are attractive but think nothing of inviting to themselves the gaze of everybody equally. In a sense I opened my eyes and came alive only after I met Mansur Ali Roedad. Before I met him, I was asleep and selfishly thought only of my own hopes and desires—my salvation. He showed me the larger picture and freed me from the painful prison of myself. What a sense of relief and expansion! I accept the role bestowed on me with whole-hearted gratitude. At the moment of truth, I should not be found wanting. But time is running out and I must hurry with this account of things because what I am trying to say here may give voice to millions of my brothers and sisters.*
>
> *Religions are modes of ordering the reality around us. Islam is not ritualistic or mystical. It is simple, clear, beautiful and unalterable. It is this last quality that the followers of other religions cannot accept. The systematic denigration and dismantling of my people's beliefs is intolerable. They watch silently with growing helplessness and desperation the armed array of invincible forces of the Western, Christian world gathering for a final onslaught*

on them. This is totally unacceptable. After Mansur showed me the movie clips I had a nightmare: Rachel is floundering in the water under a cloud of monarch butterflies and I am sitting on the edge of the water body looking on as she drowns calling out to me for help. The lake is not in America but just outside the cantonment in Sialkot or somewhere near Mansur's home town in Saudi Arabia; and Rachel's people are picnicking under a stand of palm trees oblivious to the tragedy being played out in the water just out of their sight and hearing. I do nothing because I have become sexually impotent as a prelude to becoming a complete vegetable. Mansur's disembodied voice is trying to say something to me as I sit immobile, mobbed by the butterflies that have abandoned Rachel who is going down for the third and last time.

It is impossible to sit here and keep writing when I must be getting ready to do whatever needs to be done. It was an error to believe that I could spell out anything in writing or that it would make any difference to anyone. It was just hubris to think my words would give voice to the voiceless. It is the deed and not the thought that counts. The time for action has come. Till then this must suffice, and afterwards it'll be useless.

Mother and Child: Charcoal on Charred Paper

When Rewa had a miscarriage, she started suffering from insomnia. It was in the seventh month of her first pregnancy. Until that time Rewa and Chikara had had a happy enough marriage. They were one of the numberless couples that had adopted Mumbai as their home at the height of the economic boom. Rewa was as beautiful as an answered prayer. She was a nineteen-year-old runaway when she married Chikara. Her skin was the colour of burnished copper and she had the gait and gaze of a gazelle; she was a leggy beauty with her pageboy haircut and people found it odd that she was a photographer and not a photographer's model. Chikara, who had lost his parents in a car crash on the winding hill roads of the Western Ghats near Lonavla, was hirsute, cuddly and had a winsome, tentative air about him which played on the maternal instincts of the women he came into contact with; he was a strapping fellow who was temperamentally jolly and gifted with a light-heartedness that made for an easy-going and open personality. With the loss of the baby, there was a new development: Chikara began to grind his teeth intermittently at night though he continued to sleep soundly. This only made things worse for Rewa, who now increasingly spent the larger part of every night sitting upright and wide awake in bed.

Papya Kadyan had stayed on in Mumbai after her studies making it her home base. She came from one of the outlying villages of Rohtak district in Haryana in the north and did her best to turn her back on (as she saw it) her unhappy past and forget her rural origins. She was tall, statuesque and long-necked with cascading, tar black hair. She was high-waisted with boyish hips and small breasts and no one, looking at her, would have wished her to be any more top heavy. One afternoon she bumped into Chikara coming down the granite steps of the Asiatic Society library and was so taken aback that she was momentarily speechless because he too was from Rohtak though he, unlike her, was not on the run from the ghosts of his past. They both laughed partly in recognition and partly because they were both wearing their hair in ponytails. They had met at an inter-school sports event at the Talkatora Gardens in Delhi some twelve years ago. It had been a three-day athletic meet and a happy time: both factors that facilitated nostalgic recognition. She told him in her forthright manner that she was a painter. In his own tentative fashion he avoided her eyes and said, 'I work as a journalist and Rewa, my wife, is a professional photographer. She works for an international photo agency; I mean, her work has appeared in the *National Geographic* and things like that.' He smiled in a self-deprecatory way; they exchanged pleasantries and phone numbers; and that was the extent of their first encounter in Mumbai.

When Papya got home she found a letter from Malini, her mother, waiting for her. She was irritated and mildly surprised because, for one thing, they were infrequent and poor correspondents; for another, it was no secret that Papya was not fond of her mother. When she was still in school she used to openly blame her mother for her father's disappearance. Kadyan had gone missing while Papya was still an infant, and nothing in the large store of gossip and innuendo that had filtered down to her hinted at a plausible reason for his flight. It was like magic that Kadyan should vanish without a clue as to how it happened or where he went.

Apart from a few inessential details, the letter said:

> *A stoop-shouldered stranger, who claims to be your father, has arrived here after a twenty-year absence. True, he bears a strong resemblance to your father but that could be a coincidence; he reels off dates and names events but then these things are in the public domain. He is totally incoherent, as usual, about where he has been all these years, what made him go away, and why he has chosen to come back now. The village is in a tizzy with the people shamelessly taking sides. The horror of it is he says he will publicly reveal intimate, anatomical details if that is what it takes to prove his true identity. Things are getting ugly with your aunt Shana's contention that he is the missing Kadyan who has come back to us after all these years. The worst part is that—I'm so sure of it, I might as well have seen it with my own eyes—Kadyan is sleeping with Shana in order to worm his way in, the better to make his point. Says he wants to see you. It is not that I expect you to return home or do anything in particular. I just wanted to inform you about the wretched situation developing here.*

Papya thought, if according to mother the guy is incoherent or anything else *as usual*, it must be my father; but she kept her own counsel and said nothing to her mother, waiting for the drama to play itself out.

Rewa would spend as much time as she could in the dark, rolling about sleeplessly in bed until the sound of Chikara's grinding teeth and the coagulation of shadows in the corners of the room made her put on her bedside lamp. To begin with, she doodled, scribbled and jotted down jingles and nonsense rhymes remembered from childhood. But soon she put a stop to this mirror-talk and started writing notes and memos to her unborn daughter; she hid them in various parts of the house: at least this way she felt she was communicating with someone and not talking to herself. She was so prolific she soon ran out of hiding places; every cranny was crammed with her writings and when she dragged out an old tin trunk from under the bed one day to hide her notes of the night before, she was shocked to find it jammed full with her earlier nocturnal compositions. She was a voracious reader who, in the old days, used to read herself to sleep every night which was something she now found impossible to do. Things started to go completely awry when Rewa began to rig her cameras and trip lights around the house, convinced that somehow the image of her dead child would be captured at night if she kept up her vigil and did not fall asleep. Chikara, who started tripping on the gathering junk in the house, tried in vain to confront Rewa but she could hardly be expected to explain something she herself could not understand. He soon realized the folly of trying to right things by himself. He did the round of psychiatrists and counsellors, feeding them with the bumf that was choking his marriage. They were unhelpful when not impossible. The gynaecologists turned down their suggestions that the couple try and have a baby by bluntly telling them that Rewa could never conceive again. It pained Chikara to see Rewa slide like this. She had always been a bubbly girl with a naturally sunny disposition. Mornings, Chikara himself came awake through layers of sleep, aided by two or three cups of tea and a bath, while Rewa woke up with a smile—but that was before insomnia had claimed her.

Chikara made arrangements for the two of them to get away for a week to a nearby hill station like Khandala, but Rewa insisted, for reasons he could not understand, that they go instead to Matheran. When the details were firmed up, Rewa indicated that she would prefer to go all the way by road. It had nothing to do with his parent's deaths but Chikara hated travelling on those winding hill roads. For Rewa's sake he cancelled the train tickets and organized the necessary road transport. When the taxi was at the door, there was a phone call from Papya asking Chikara for some information. Chikara told her that Rewa and he were going away for a week and he promised to get in touch with her directly on their return. In answer to Rewa's question he told her about Papya and though there was not much that he had to say, in her troubled state, Rewa said, 'I hope she's not one of those women who will end up by coming between us.'

Matheran was crawling with the usual crowd from Mumbai and there were the usual pastimes like the walk along the mall; the police band played music in the evenings in the open rotunda in the marketplace. There were the usual crowds at the skating rink, the pricey food joints and the converted opera house showing popular Hindi films; as Rewa said, 'It is no great shakes but it's good fun for a change.' But here too, in spite of the distractions of a new place, the mornings found Rewa curled up in exhaustion and Chikara hunting for further fragments of letters to their unborn daughter that would never need to be posted. Even though Chikara had packed Rewa's camera, they returned from the hills with no photographic memento of their holiday.

The most unexpected improvement in Rewa came about as a direct result of her meeting with Papya on their return to Mumbai. Rewa unburdened herself to Papya as never before and felt a sense of such relief for the first time in months that she fell fast asleep after their long chat. The strange thing was that not only did Papya display an infinite capacity to take in what Rewa had to say, but she told her about the complex situation evolving, even as they spoke, in her village—a thing she had not mentioned to anyone before; in fact Rewa fixed on the details of that far-fetched drama with such avidity that she completely lost track of her own problems. Chikara heard for the first time of Papya's problems in bits and driblets from Rewa.

Rewa and Papya took to meeting in places like the Chemold and Jehangir art galleries, restaurants and seminar halls and exchanged information with an intensity that transformed it into intimacy.

Papya presented Rewa with one of her recent oil paintings entitled 'Mother and Child'. It depicted a crowded scene in which naked men and women seemed to be inextricably tangled together under the branches of a grove of oak trees; the foliage of each tree in the composition was strangely divided with half the leaves painted blue and the other half green. It was a sombre picture, where every hue seemed to assume a darker shade when moving from palette to canvas. The light in the picture was unequally distributed, illuminating certain areas and leaving others in shadows of different densities because of the dappled sunlight. Each time Rewa studied the painting, she was inexorably drawn to something that was happening, not in the foreground or background but in the middle distance: slightly to the left of centre, in the welter of bodies a woman, bent at the waist, was suckling an infant while at the same time, a misshapen old man in a yellow turban and with a very long beard was penetrating her from behind. It was a mottled part of the painting (except for the splash of yellow) which revealed itself only to a close observer.

Rewa and Papya got used to the constant smell of paint and turpentine; they went shopping for art books and photographic materials together; Rewa made herself an expert in dealing with the carpenters who framed the pictures and stretched the canvases at Papya's place. They frequented restaurants located in large, anonymous hotels where they booked into rooms for weekends or took to visiting their friends like Shirin Contractor or Clythie Fernandes. To begin with Chikara, noting his wife's sudden and radical improvement, had encouraged the frequency of her meetings with Papya but he was left standing still by the sheer speed at which events seemed to overtake, even overwhelm, him. He helplessly looked on as Rewa regained her effervescent self and slipped away from him into Papya's arms.

As the situation in his house worsened, with Chikara sleeping (when he was not lying awake like Rewa before him) in the drawing room and hardly getting to exchange a word with her for days together, he took to staying away from home for longer and longer periods, working early and late in office and boozing at the press club with those very colleagues for whom he had earlier felt a degree of contempt exactly because they drank to drown their domestic difficulties much as he felt he was now driven to do. Even when he was tanked up he could hold his liquor well but nowadays, he seemed abstracted, permanently absent where he stood. On compassionate grounds his office sympathetically considered his request for a transfer and posted him to Delhi. What happened was this: one day, as he was idly going through a drawer stuffed with Rewa's nocturnal outpourings, he came upon something that threw him. Among the crumpled papers he happened upon Rewa's hidden photographs of Papya in the nude. He found himself suddenly attracted to Papya as never before. So strong was her pulling power that his immediate reaction was to step backwards and away. This, in fact, was the proximate cause of his sudden decision to abandon Mumbai. When he moved to Delhi he took with him his office-related papers, educational certificates and a minimum of his essential personal effects (like the woven reed mat on which he did his yoga), leaving behind his music system, most of his clothes and all his books. He had always felt that Rewa was more of a bookworm than he was.

Overnight, he reinvented himself as a political correspondent in Delhi and, oiled with alcohol and self-pity, he expertly navigated his way between the bureaucrats and powerbrokers who clogged the arteries of the capital. The junk food in Delhi is quite different from the stuff available in Mumbai. He was a street food freak and since pushcart fare is different from locality to locality, he particularly missed Mumbai whenever he was hungry; but this and other such longings in him only pointed to the fact that he was learning to be alone.

The instant Chikara left for Delhi, Papya moved in with Rewa. She did not give up her old flat though. As Rewa started picking up and knitting the unravelled threads of her past life she happily found that both her office work and her photography were more satisfying and far more financially rewarding than ever before. Papya invited Rewa to join her in doing up her old flat as a studio-cum-darkroom for their common use; Rewa readily agreed to help with the renovation work but she insisted that she just didn't want a darkroom there for herself because she already had access to one in her office. While redoing the place, Papya told Rewa, 'You have the uncommon ability to step back from your work. In my line of country that is what makes all the difference between just a good painter and a truly great artist.' They had good fun decorating the old place. While Rewa worked longer and longer at the studio, Papya took it upon herself, at Rewa's suggestion, to spring clean their living quarters. Papya gave the old place a thorough cleaning and in the process recovered all the letters, notes and memos, not lost or destroyed, which Rewa had written and hidden; she also collected the photographs that Chikara had not tampered with, which lay interleaved with all the other stuff. She sifted, filed and carefully moved them to her studio. It had never occurred to Chikara to do what Papya did: read them. She did not attempt to categorize or analyse those black symbols on white paper, born of an unquenchable thirst for the child that was irrecoverably lost. With no preconceptions she took in the details as they came, slowly and naturally until, like a just-finished painting, they yielded a picture wherein she saw Rewa's naked need in all its colours for what it really was and suggested to her that they should adopt a girl child. That night as she was falling asleep, Rewa decided that she was intensely happy—happy and effete like one who has just given birth to a child after hard labour. The next few days they were in high spirits, running around learning how to adopt a baby.

The day of the first rains of the monsoon, Rewa was late getting away from office. On arriving home she found Papya sitting on the couch in front of the TV wearing one of Chikara's old shirts. That night, as the city was pelted by the incessant rain, they lay together, completely relaxed, their bodies smelling of each other, when Rewa sleepily mumbled into Papya's ear, 'The clothes thing is not necessary, you know. We don't need it.' Papya, who had her hand across Rewa's hip, didn't say anything but just patted the small of her back in lieu of having to agree or disagree with her. Papya took to wearing Chikara's jogging shoes and track suits to her studio. She cut her long hair to shoulder length just like Chikara and wore it in a ponytail. She bought herself a pair of Ray Ban shades like the one he had had and took to wearing it everywhere and at all times even if only on her head.

One languorous August afternoon, Papya rang up Rewa and asked her if she was in the mood for a hot drink of some description and when she agreed to it Papya suggested that they meet at the Wayside Inn at the Kala Ghoda. It had been a favourite haunt of Chikara's where he loved to hang out, dipping his buttered toast in his tea and talking shop with his cronies for whom this was virtually a home away from the Press Club.

Back in the village the police had been brought in to identify 'Kadyan'. His fingerprints and dental records were sent to faraway places to be checked. At this precise point in time, when no definitive identification had as yet been made by the police, Malini did a Kadyan on the whole lot by disappearing without a trace. Even 'Kadyan', who could give no coherent account of his own absence, was at a complete loss as to Malini's possible whereabouts. The only possible lead was the story, spreading like a rumour in the bazaar, that a tall, bearded stranger with a mane of shaggy, long hair was seen talking to Malini over the hedge that bordered her back courtyard. However, this was considered dubious evidence as the witness was said to be a drunkard, and even the cops discounted it as a serious lead on the ground that the description of the man was obviously melodramatic enough to have been made up. In this changed context, 'Kadyan' asked Shana to write to Papya about the latest developments in the case and asked the police to stop their investigations into his identity. But this only complicated the case further because investigations, once set in motion, gain a momentum all their own and cannot be cut short; also, interest now zeroed in on 'Kadyan' as the prime suspect in the disappearance of Malini.

To begin with, Papya spent more time in the studio pouring over Rewa's writings than doing her own work. But her true love of painting saved her from the wasteland of words she was wandering into. Soon she returned to the canvas and the easel in the studio with such renewed vigour that her paintings started commanding wider critical attention and higher prices in the market. But she continued to sift through Rewa's discarded writings because of a singular occurrence: she happened upon a piece of writing of such incandescent beauty and of such an unlikely provenance that she could not help thinking that it was a supernatural manifestation. She pieced it together from three separate fragments torn from a single sheet of paper and crumpled into a dirty ball. It was about a prostitute and her dead baby stumbling across the border from Syria to Iraq as victims of the collateral damage of the war in the Middle East, entitled 'Charcoal on Charred Paper':

> *It is not Karbala. It is not Muharram. And the mad woman with the dead child is not even a Shia. She drifts down the twisting alley with the infant draped across her shoulder like a towel. Grief forces her down the insistent passage, her footsteps tracing a pattern on the path that mimics a damask design in her unhinged head. It can't be just the sun. The pedestrians—mostly men—separate and make way for her blind progress. But she is not blind. The others can see and recognize death and the sighted even at a distance. They are merely bystanders and passers-by killing time or telling the beads they've been told to tell. This time it is a mother with her lifeless offspring: a picture bled white of all colour in the blinding glare. It's commonplace now. It's just the war. It's nothing. Most of them turn away. The others take in the scene with half-closed eyes as if they had seen it all before, times without number.*
>
> *It is the very height of summer in a backstreet skirting the tomb of a Sufi saint with the open sewer dribbling into the wadi on one side and the rubble and gutted shops on the other side; most of them are butcheries and idle lathe-machine workshops. The smoke from the wood fires keeps close to the ground and moves horizontally around this*

old quarter of a bombed border town in Iraq, far from the brothel on the road to Damascus where, as a child herself, she was first abused. Unsullied by the depravity pressing on her on all sides, she has been moved from house to house, not one of which was a home to her. The flayed, rosy carcasses of consumable animals, quick with flies, hang in generous portions from iron hooks. Kites and vultures riding the thermals, on the constant lookout for the dead and dying, wheel through the incredibly blue sky. Inviolate, she moves through the crowd of unmoved watchers, a mirage wobbling in the heat haze or just a ghost at noon, touching no one in her wake.

She moves forward with mincing steps in time to an air inaudible to all but her, as if in precise synchrony with a phalanx of other dancers. But she is alone. Weeping and wailing she beats her breasts rhythmically. She passes by—a mourning sleepwalker moving in measure like a male Muharram dancer in a penitential procession in Karbala—bearing the unbearable weight of her dead child as though it weighs nothing at all.

It seemed to Papya more like a lyric or a sonata—a magical composition; and she could not stop wondering if the words and images of Shia Islam in customary celebration of Muharram in the holy city of faraway Karbala had come to Rewa in a dream as consolation or a balm to keep her from going insane in her grief in the dead of night as she struggled to cope with her sense of total loss next to her sleeping husband. It was a discovery that made her abandon some of the more obvious character aspects of Chikara that she found herself borrowing recently. Not that she was looking for any incendiary material, but however many times she went through the accumulated mass of material she did not find anything that set her on fire like the mother-and-child piece entitled 'Charcoal on Charred Paper'. Never for a single moment did she question the actuality of the event. She was haunted by it. She did manage though to salvage several pieces of Rewa's writings, many of them with a beginning, a middle and an end each; they were in completely different keys and, if she didn't know better, she may well have considered them the work of many hands.

As she ordered the material before her, she and Rewa did the rounds of agencies and non-governmental organizations involved in facilitating child adoption work connected to hospitals and orphanages. They filled in forms and applications and provided the mandatory requirements like proof of residence, financial solvency and so on. It was a long-winded process and required patience above other things; it was a quality that Rewa had in short supply but luckily for them, Papya more than made up for it. After an endless amount of waiting they were informed that in six months their long wait would be over. As a way to minimize Rewa's fretfulness Papya suggested that they take a long holiday—against all common sense and the considered advice of well-wishers—in war-torn Iraq. Rewa saw no connection between the writings of her insomniac nights and real life; she certainly had no memory of or connection to them; she simply agreed to the Iraqi holiday without asking Papya why she had decided on Iraq of all places. Later she said, 'I think I know why you want to go there.'

'Why?' asked Papya, patting her hair and adjusting her dark glasses on her head.

'Because Iraq is still a country laid waste by war. You once said that that is where it all began. Not life—that was in Africa. You meant civilization.'

'Yes,' said Papya with something like relief, for she was quite unclear about her own motives. 'After all, we are not going there in search of safety.'

The summer had been a scorcher in Delhi and now it was pushing towards the end of August and still there was no sign of rain. Word of Papya and Rewa's planned Iraqi sojourn and the proposed child adoption had spread through friends and common acquaintances from Mumbai to Delhi. Chikara mentioned the news to Malini in his non-committal way. Malini heard him out in silence with her head bowed and her face in shadow. Chikara clawed his way out of the hole he found himself in. He did not binge and hit the bottle hard any more. He eased up on drinking spirits and hard liquor and found that he quite enjoyed swilling chilled beer particularly in the heat wave conditions that prevailed in Delhi. His new look was helped along by the fact that now, after his meeting with Malini in Rohtak, he had shaved off his beard and wore his hair cut short. He seemed to be a changed person. His colleagues attributed the whole thing to the break-up of his marriage. Whatever may have passed between Malilni and himself, she was now ensconced in his house, hidden from public gaze and shame and very slowly coming face to face with her true self for the first time in her life. Chikara saw in her lovely face the lineaments of the girl she must have earlier been, overlaid with the lines of rejection that tangled her life.

Chikara tried to spend as much time with Malini as possible, for both their sakes. In some ways it was like having his mother back and as far as Malini was concerned, he represented the son she'd never had. At her suggestion he started working out in the gym prior to doing his yoga. Soon the pinched look on his face disappeared. Both Malini and he found they enjoyed listening to old Hindi film songs on the world space radio and watching old black-and-white movies on the video at home. He gave up reading books, more or less, concentrating only on the newspapers and political periodicals. He hurried home to Malini who had lost her vague air of being permanently injured because she had now found a new focus and purpose in life, in caring for Chikara who dramatically responded by losing his flab and looking more centred than ever before. In the afternoons, in the empty house, she would give the go-by to the bed in her own room on the other side of the drawing room and spread out Chikara's mat in the balcony; she would lie there on her side, resting her head on her bent arm, inhaling the musky odour of Chikara's perspiration emanating from the mat and gazing at the passing traffic below with half-closed eyes. At such moments she was invaded, as never before, by a deep sense of peace.

Papya and Rewa were kept busy preparing for their Iraqi trip. Largely at the instigation of Papya, they quite rightly decided that this was no ordinary holiday and accordingly made meticulous preparations for it. They hunted in consulates and libraries and obtained maps and information brochures that they studied with the same attention to detail as they had their adoption papers. When their travel documents were being readied, more than one person at the consulate told them, 'The war may be over but the killings are on. Don't go there now.' Postpone your trip, they said, but Papya and Rewa were adamant. They were interested in

Iraq today, not tomorrow. We are not tourists, they said; we are not going there in search of security. Papya had a special, a secret interest: she wanted to pin down the exact location on the piece of real estate where the mother-and-child dream episode had played itself out.

Even at the airport in Baghdad, there were the unmistakable signs of the conflicts of the recent past like the mangled and burnt-out carcass of a bus that had smashed through the guardrails and lay rusting in the shrubs and licorice bushes or the unfilled bomb crater beside the road. The sun beat down on a flat and dusty city scarred by war. Hungry for experience, Papya and Rewa took in everything they could see along the road to Mosul in the north, pointing out to each other the date palms, the citrus trees and the poplars, the buzzards and vultures in the sky or the shy sand grouse that put in a rare appearance. Rewa was busy making a photographic record of their whole trip while Papya confined herself to her sketchbooks. Most of their nights were spent in lamplight, candlelight or darkness because of the power cuts and outages. It was a sweet, water-poor country where there was no electricity at all during the daytime. One day their rickety bus stopped beside a grove of valonia oak trees whose trunks had been stripped of their bark for tanning leather (they were told). The leaves of these trees were half blue and half green. Under the largest oak sat a very small, misshapen old man in a yellow turban, with a beard that was longer than him (Rewa was disturbed at finding him vaguely familiar but unidentifiable); some of the passengers went up to the soothsayer to have their fortunes told. Rewa and Papya were about to turn back for the bus when the old man called out to them. He said, 'Rewa. Papya', and gestured to them to come closer. His young sidekick signalled to them to come closer even more vigorously by waving his arms. They were shocked that a stranger in this strange land should know their names. But he allowed them no time for questions or surprise and pushed a stack of pages with writing on them in Arabic, Sanskrit, Hebrew, Chinese, Roman and other scripts. He riffled the pages like a cardsharp and asked Rewa to pick a page. As it happened, it contained a single line in English: PRAYER IS THE ONLY ANSWER.

He snatched the page out of her hand before they could understand what it was all about and waving both his arms at them for emphasis and urgency, he shouted and his interpreter shouted even louder, 'Go home. Go home.' And for good measure he added, 'I am not one of your riff-raff from around these parts like Erbil or Diyala. Your money I don't want. I come from the southern marshes where grow the reeds. Forget Iraq. Go home.'

Their passage through Iraq was of a piece; there was disturbing evidence wherever they went of the vulnerability of a country at odds with itself; and yet all the want and suffering could not mask the warm generosity of a baffled people driven to the edge of their very existence and beyond. Their hosts would invariably put before them a few dates from their meagre rations. Papya and Rewa gifted their photos and drawings which were received with gratitude. In Najaf they were treated to a musical afternoon with oud and rebab while a ferocious dust storm partially buried the house they were huddled in. Parts of the south seemed strangely different with backwaters, creeks and marshes; there was no hunt here for shade and moisture—not at all like the rest of the sandy country baking in the sun. The sounds of bombs and gunfire were never far away though; it was general all over Iraq.

Not discounting the niggling difficulties, it was an immensely successful, even if dangerous, holiday. Both the women had lost a considerable amount of weight. But strangely, in spite of this and the minor illnesses they were plagued by, both of them seemed to be energized and focused. They were very happy with the way things had gone so far and when Papya proposed that they visit the small towns close to the Syrian border, Rewa readily agreed. They scoured these small towns looking for the tomb of a nameless Sufi saint. The place was pullulating with refugees streaming in the general direction of Syria looking for the sanctuary of secure borders and boundaries that existed only in their heads. The roadsides hereabouts were choked with tents and makeshift shanties. The people in these small border communities laughed at them when they asked if there was a Sufi tomb anywhere nearby. You want Sufi, they said, then go on the road to Damascus; here only death. Rewa went along with Papya unquestioningly, like a child accompanying a parent. One of them was chasing a dream that the other had dreamt and long forgotten. Rewa, going through her photos, was shocked to find that cumulatively they were a telling record of a country wasted by war. Papya never did manage to identify the border town that had thrown up an indelible image of the dance of death where the footsteps of the mother driven mad with grief at the loss of her child was forever graven on her heart. They were nearing their journey's end. The things they had experienced in a few days in Iraq seemed to make their lives fuller than all that they had done and packed into their past lives earlier—because death was at their elbow all the time.

In Delhi Malini found herself in Chikara's bedroom comforting and being comforted by him in ways unfamiliar to both of them; they were grateful for the lack of light in which each thought only of the other's need. That very night, back in Baghdad, Papya was woken up by the soft sounds of Rewa sobbing. 'It was the sight of those tiny bodies swaddled in white cloth.' She was sitting up in bed, resting her forehead on her drawn-up knees. Earlier in the day they had witnessed the funeral procession of five children who had died because of a bomb blast in a school. 'In spite of all the pain, poverty and death I would not have missed this journey for anything. You do believe me, don't you? I am stronger now and richer in the things that count. We really have learned so much, haven't we?' she sobbed, shaking Papya's shoulder. 'Yes,' said Papya, 'Yes. Hush. Go to sleep now. Sleep.'

They did not get much sleep that night and were ready to leave at the break of day. Rewa and Papya stood beside an ill-assorted group of foreigners waiting for the airport bus. In the raw, early morning light they could see their bus coughing and slowly making its way towards them from the direction of the flea market at the foot of the bridge, past the makeshift vegetable and fruit stalls which were being assembled for the day. When their baggage was safely stowed away and the passengers, to a person, settled down to a breakfast of dried fruit and biscuits, the bomb in the bus was detonated. The explosion blew the bus apart, instantaneously killing its occupants.

It was quite some time before the news reached home. There were tears in Malini's eyes, not for her daughter who had been blown to smithereens but for the waif of a hulk who had burrowed his face in her lap like any upset child nuzzling its mother. She made no attempt to wipe her streaming cheeks but continued to rhythmically run her fingers through his hair as his sobbing slowed down and his shoulders ceased heaving spasmodically.

Winter Solstice

He met her for the first time when she was twenty-three years of age and he was an ageing rake. It was during one of those long waits for a connecting flight in the airport on a crisp December night. It was that peculiar time of dusk which lasts longer than a lifetime or, indeed, several lifetimes. He was sitting in one of those plastic chairs alongside the glass wall of the airport, bored. He was waiting, with the stems of his reading glasses laced between the fingers of his hands that rested on the unread newspaper spread out on his lap, when he became aware of this girl who stood next to the drinking water fountain trying to set her lovely face to rights. Her sensitive face seemed to suggest she had just that minute stopped sobbing in secret. She was wearing jeans and a grass-green kurta with an earth-coloured, open waistcoat, her jacket and scarf half sticking out of the tote bag at her side. Her straight, black hair, piled upon her head, seemed to be held in place with what looked like a lacquered chopstick.

As he took in the scene, he had difficulty breathing as though he had suddenly reached an altitude wanting in oxygen. He had more time than he knew what to do with and as he sat gawking at her, she dropped her handbag. Her eyeliner rolled very, very slowly down the floor towards his shoe; she followed its progress towards him without picking up her purse or its scattered contents; their eyes met when the eyeliner came to a stop and they both broke into smiles. Just then, bright lights came on in the airport as he picked up her eyeliner. She did not come right away to claim it though. She went down on her knees and took her time examining in detail each of the items that had fallen out of her bag as though that would restore something of their former sheen to them. As she bent down, her hair came undone and the whole silken mass cascaded and bounced down her slender shoulders. She came to him when she was done with picking up her things and sat down in the chair next to him and said, 'Thanks a ton,' before extending her hand towards him for her eyeliner while at the same time looking past him at something that was happening there beyond the glass wall behind him. Over tea, in the upstairs restaurant, he tried to draw her out while suppressing his own awkward eagerness; there was the constant roar of planes landing and taking off. She kept putting up her hair so lackadaisically that it kept tumbling down repeatedly; and each time she put her arms up, her kurta sleeves slid back and he could see the green veins beneath her translucent skin. The aspect of her girlish beauty he was most attracted to was the contradictory sadness in her sparkling eyes: inky pools of promise and sorrow from which there seemed to be no possible way out. She did not respond to his question as to whether she was a frequent traveller but, like one who spurned small talk in departure lounges, she asked, 'Are you a married man?'

'I was married, I am told,' he said, 'but that was a very long time ago.'

'Divorced or widowed?' She looked out at the gathering darkness illumined here and there with the airport lights.

'Neither,' he said, and left the matter dangling in the air, groping for a response. Unable to decide on what might be a suitable answer he told her the truth; he told her that he had lost his memory one day and with it his entire past. He was out on the road when it happened. He could remember nothing prior to that; though there were leftover bits and pieces reported to him, they did not add up to a pathway into the past. 'I've heard that I was married, with family. Were there sons and daughters? How many of them were there? I know nothing. People just say these things without a thought. However, a man in my position cannot give credence to such stories that are bound to follow him all the time.' What he did know about his past after the incident on the road was that his sex life was limited to prostitutes. It had been an easy way out. It was a preference that went a long way towards explaining his socially inept shyness in the presence of feminine company.

'Tell me the earliest thing you remember,' she said, with genuine interest. She knew that he was smitten with her from the moment she saw him drink her in with his hungry gaze; he seemed to have great difficulty in tearing his eyes away from her, even momentarily. This stranger, who was old enough to belong to her mother's generation, wanted her. She knew it in the pit of her stomach. It had never been like this with boys of her own age who kept pestering her to go out with them. Looking back, they suddenly seemed like callow youths not worthy of her attention. The man seated before her though was a mature person who seemed a little lost in her perfumed presence. This made him awkward in his responses; and she too, like others before her, mistook it for innocence and inexperience. She found his account of amnesia so seductive partly because she had never heard of such a thing before, partly because nothing is more alluring than correctly reading the effects of one's own attraction in the eyes of another, and partly because it seemed to stir something in her past. 'Tell me the first thing you remember about yourself and I'll tell you my earliest memories,' she promised with a smile.

'It was early Sunday morning in winter and I was on the road,' he said. 'I was wearing my tracksuit and my trainers, no watch or wallet. I was exhausted as though I had covered miles and miles on foot; maybe I had. I have not talked about this matter to anyone; I have not talked about it even to myself. Forgive me if I stumble or digress. I remember that misty, first day when I forgot everything with painful clarity. I did not know who I was or where I came from. I was so tired I thought I would drop dead. I was grimy and exhausted, as if I had been travelling for days on end. Where did I start out from? What was it that triggered such a complete and final memory loss in me? These are only some of the many unanswered questions on which my life is built. After that, it was a long, slow haul that had all the earmarks of an ordinary and uneventful life. That is the boring truth.'

'You know, my father left us before I was born,' she said, keeping her part of the bargain as she saw it. 'The story goes that he went missing and did not leave behind him a single clue as to his motives or whereabouts. Luckily for us, my mother was a professional journalist; but even with her connections, she could make no headway in tracing my missing father through all the years of my growing up. Over the passing years, I think she went through the motions as a matter of form. She had managed to fashion her personal life quite comfortably around his absence from as far back as I can remember. Even as she lay dying of cancer three years ago, her last thoughts were not of my father but herself.' She made a face.

The teapot was refilled and he stirred the contents with a spoon, to her mild amusement. Perhaps it was his age or intensity or a combination of the two that pointed to his incongruous desire for the wonderful creature before him. Whatever the reason for her bemusement, it did not diminish his growing ardour for her. While she was absorbed in watching the operation, he caught her in an unguarded moment for the first time since their coming together; and he saw a hint in her lovely face of a likeness to himself that passed like a hunter's shadow on the uneven, granite walls of ancestral caves in the past beneath layers of his conscious mind. It was an ancient and inchoate image of such pressing import that it was well beyond the persistence of human vision; and though it was only an unformed thought that precluded the possibility of any recognition, it was clearly a warning from the gods.

They were both new to this kind of thing: trying to put part of their past into words. In order to minimize the strangeness he felt, he began making up things as he went along. He said, 'I am essentially a travelling man. On the move, I feel free. Too long in any one place and I begin to feel hemmed in, almost helpless. In transit all places are mere passing shows; always on the move like that, I am not limited or defined by either the station I have left behind me or the next terminus I am headed towards. You could say I am like a man on the run. What am I running away from? Myself, of course.' Getting carried away he laughed sheepishly. 'But enough about me. Tell me about your father.'

She too found herself opening up as never before in front of this old man who wanted to possess her with his whole being. 'My father's disappearance from our lives,' she said, 'was the ground reality of my childhood. Everything was measured by that constant absence which seemed to dictate most of my mother's strategies and my girlish subterfuges: A dinner for a visiting brother would, in her telling, blossom into a party for her absent husband's non-existent friend; or it would be that old chestnut about him being temporarily away because of his work in the merchant navy. I too made up imaginary friends to converse with, telling these fictional characters lies about the gifts my father had bought me from his travels abroad. My mother's journalistic work often kept her away from home and it was during these periods of aloneness in my childhood that I surrounded myself with my make-believe friends. These ploys and other such feints were all very well but I now approach the dark area of my life that I have never been able to drag into the clear light of day—it concerns my mother's affairs with other men.' She took a deeper than normal breath and when he looked into her face, he saw that her eyes had assumed a drowning, inward gaze that drew him into their dark, tangled depths.

'Once,' she continued in a voice that rang and resonated in his ears, 'I had gone over to my friend, Shika's place, to look her up when she was down with flu. They lived quite close to us and Shika was my best friend at the time. I left Shika on the bed and went into the drawing room to get her the atlas she insisted on showing me. I could not help but overhear the conversation conducted in stage whispers over the common wall of the kitchen balcony between Shika's mother and their next-door neighbour—a woman with a withered arm. Shika's mother, who did most of the talking, was holding the other's wasted arm in both her hands even though they seemed to be pulling away from each other. I was careful not to be caught peeking through the bead curtain separating the kitchen from the drawing room. It immediately struck me, as I listened to the words—most of which, to begin with, I did not catch or understand—that they were talking about my mother. "She can't help herself, poor thing." "Not after the way he left her, without so much as a by your leave." "Naturally. I am not blaming her. Such people, I am told, cannot really control themselves. Everything will fall on that poor girl's back; she's with Shika now," with a shake of the head in the direction of the bedroom. "She'll be unfit for human company—what do you expect?" "With a mother like that, setting her an example like that." "Hopeless; hopeless."'

She paused in her narration and looked up directly into his eyes. He presented the figure of a caring person who had barricaded himself from emotional contact and starved himself of human company. She of course had no way of knowing that this was only a very small part of the whole picture. The word waif rose to her mind and her heart went out to him. Just then, an intervening silence ensued between them. It was a defining moment and as he thought of her with tender lust she, instinctively believing in the prophylactic properties of pouring her heart out to a sympathetic stranger, continued with her confession: 'There are times when I have often wondered what it was that I resented more, my father's nagging absence or my lax mother's presence? In the beginning I paid no attention to her frequent visits to the family doctor. Once when she had sprained her ankle badly, he paid us a house call. She seemed suddenly younger in his presence, patting her hair and laughing excessively at his casual remarks as if they were witty pronouncements; it was as if the air around her was suddenly charged with the promise of fun times. These things did not seem to add up to much in those early days; it was only later and that too very, very slowly that I sensed them coming together. One day, I returned home early and unannounced from college. But just before entering the house with my latchkey, I stopped short because I thought I heard voices in the house—my mother's voice was high and girlish, laced with laughter. Though my mother did not keep regular hours in her journalistic work, she was never at home in the forenoon; she was not a light-hearted person normally, though a coquettish laughter did seem to escape her when she found herself in the presence of men who seemed attracted to her. I turned away from home and headed for the college library where I spent the whole day working, only to return home late that evening. I asked her, after dinner that night, if she had managed to go to the Old Customs Office as she had planned to. "I spent the whole boring morning there," she lied, "sorting through the rubbish that is so dear to the politicos; still I can't really complain as my editor is as pleased as punch with the whole affair."'

His scheduled flight was announced but he said he would give it a miss and take a later one that night. 'Once, on an impulse, my friends and I decided to take in an exhibition on handcrafted jewellery in one of the posh hotels in the city centre,' she said. It seemed she just could not stop herself from going on about her mother's inconstancy. 'There, in the lobby, as we were passing between the arcaded shops on either side, I happened to see a couple in a clinch in a kiosk draped with shawls: it was my mother with a man I did not recognize. Do I go on about this too much? Yes, yes, I know I do. There were several such episodes and I have never spoken about them to anybody—not even myself. I kept my own counsel in total silence through the years of my growing up. My mother's friendships were never a topic of conversation between us. But it was a silence that played a larger part in moulding our relationship than anything we ever said to each other, much as our lives were essentially shaped less by those who were present around us than by my father's formative absence.'

With trepidation he hoped that this would be the first of many other meetings between them. He hoped that they would most probably begin by going out to take in some movies and plays, then there would be plays and dinners. And then there would be the long, slow dinners that would be a prelude to the short, frenetic stays in hotels in out-of-the-way places in the city or in the small towns just outside the municipal limits. It was the familiar world of his nightlife into which he wanted to draw her. Their getting together was bound to be frenzied and hectic. That was how he saw this encounter playing itself out. 'Look,' she said, as he came out of his lustful reverie. 'I've never seen so many stars in a winter sky. Do you think we'll have frost tonight?' The glow of warm well-being that emanated from her as she looked outside the glass partition reached out to him.

Insomnia

Bitia was a ghost. She entered Benaras one moonless night like a song in search of a singer. Every single thing in Benaras was calculated to ensnare a ghost like Bitia. Allured and seduced by its cooking, body, gutter, rotting and burning smells, Bitia, like any other casual passer-by, was turned into a semi-permanent fixture in Benaras. Like those with nothing to lose, like those who go there to find something but find quite something other, like those who continue to stay on there till the sweet end, forgetting their bitter beginnings and the reason they set out for that place, in the first place . . .

Professionally, Bitia was a photographer. She had sparkling eyes and raven black hair that came down to her knees. Her sloe eyes were pools of pain whose changing depths strangely hinted at the promise of happiness. One moment it was there, the next it was gone—it was not a quality that could be pinned down. There, in that city of cities, she was repeatedly abused. But every depravity heaped upon her only made her purer and more radiant. The more she was degraded, the more youthful she became; and even those who sought to defile her were made whole and clean.

Bitia looked around at the huddled figures bent over the dung fires in the terracotta landscape and the clotted forms in the shadows patiently waiting out the interminable night; the darkness was unequally scattered by the naphtha flares, the burning ghats where the funeral pyres were burning and the neon lights. There were long lines of the dead waiting to be burned. She studied the available light that was diffuse and irregular. Being a moonless night, the sky had no tonal quality at all. She stood still and closed her eyes, and the pain of the pulsing city seeped into her blood like toxin. Bitia took a room on the roof with an outside spiral staircase that led up to her balcony, which overlooked the potter's colony. There, the red earth and dirty but holy water were combined to make the pots in which small quantities of the sacred Ganga water were transported to other less providentially blessed regions of the earth.

If you make your living from the dead, there is no place like Benaras. More people go there to die than to live; to die there ensures an escape from the endless cycle of birth and rebirth. There was a great demand for Brahmin priests like Shastri who officiated at several cremations a day or Jara, the low-caste dom who prepared the dead bodies for the funeral pyres. They were just two of the numberless people transformed by their intimate contact with Bitia—who cast no shadow, who left no footprints, who married Shastri but spent her nights with that untouchable, Jara, and other outcasts and rejects; she was there to save the lost and the hopeless.

Unlike the other priests, Shastri did not submit himself to fasting, flogging or fire-walking. When they first met, Shastri saw or thought he saw fleetingly a spirit of fierce independence in Bitia but what he said to her was that she had a face that was both sorrowful and sensitive. He could not get over the chromatic picture she made against the dusky window and she knew it. Shastri, much older than her, was a widower. But nothing in his temperament or training had prepared him for this encounter. It was a Sunday evening in winter.

'So I look as sad as Sunday?' she asked him with a smile, repeating what he had just said. The shadows in her eyes shifted and her face lit up. He was in thrall to the magic of her beauty as only a person who is hopelessly in love can be. He laughed in response and looked out of the window. It was not love nor the melancholy scene outside though, where the street lamps had just come on and were clashing against the failing light in the sky, but her lying words that felled him—she told him that she was pregnant—just like that, out of nowhere. Her words hung in the air, with nothing leading up to them or away from them. It was then that Shastri broke the silence and asked her if she would marry him and she agreed.

Jara was in his late teens when Bitia, nearly twice his age, first invited him to go with her to her room on the roof that she used as a studio-cum-darkroom. It was a balmy summer night. Jara was minding the bodies burning on the Manikarnika Ghat. It was his duty to keep vigil and see to it that no one pinched the firewood or the pots in which the ashes were collected for immersion in the Ganga. It was his responsibility to prevent people from taking photographs. There were always visitors about wanting to capture these cremations on film—hordes of camera-ready foreign tourists. Bitia was dying to show him her photographs, initiate him into the mystery of sex, and teach him photography. The night was full of the settled cacophony of devotional noises at cross-purposes with one another when Bitia's whispered invitation to Jara rose from behind a stack of firewood, uncontaminated by the sepsis of sanctity all round, and set him on the road to manhood.

The half-light of the street lamps barely spilled into the room. Bitia hit Jara with her body like a palpable dream. She made love to him with the meticulous frenzy of the incorporeal. Later, she showed him stacks of photographs she had taken in Benaras; many of them were of funeral pyres and he featured, to his amusement, in several of them. He returned to his cadavers before dawn, his eyes jammed with after-images of Bitia, his whole being suffused with the perfume from her hair.

Bitia avoided sunlight as much as possible, saying the glare gave her a migraine. She moved adroitly with an amazing economy of movement and grace from one patch of shade to another in the dappled sunlight without casting even a mottled shadow. It was very difficult to pin her down during the daytime; she was always somewhere else. And yet, people seemed to accept her as one of their own. Whenever she could not be found, there was always talk of her being seen at the dhobi ghat where the washermen were beating the clothes; or she was outside the Ganesha shrine, rolling cotton wicks for the earthen oil lamps; others reported seeing her with a group of women singing hymns to that rutting, blue god, Krishna. After she moved into Shastri's house, Bitia got rid of all the mirrors. Once after the rains, Shastri called her out into the garden to look at a diesel oil rainbow in a puddle of water. She looked into the water with her face next to his but agitated the water with her fingers and rushed back into the house before he could notice the absence of her reflection in the water. It was just a reflex action on her part, because, by then, Shastri knew that she was a ghost—the ghost he loved.

Bitia was besotted with Benaras. She taught Jara the rudiments of photography, using the minimum number of words. Generally, she was silent and hardly ever had a word for Jara. But whenever she was with Shastri, she talked endlessly—often all night long, always about Benaras. Shastri could never have enough of her or her words. He adored her even though he was well aware that he had only a minuscule part of her with him; he knew only too well that she was—even at that very moment—elsewhere, intensely pursuing her several separate lives beyond his human reach.

Once he had asked her, 'But why Benaras? Why this city crammed with beggars? What is it that grabs you about this city?'

'This city, like me, never sleeps. What I see in Benaras is transfigured before my very eyes, and this, in turn, makes me more forgiving. That's why I adore this merciful place.'

Over the years Jara took many photographs of Bitia but she never appeared in a single one of them. She was neither a silhouette nor a blank cutout—very simply, there was no outline. Her absence in the photographic record was total, complete.

Bitia, of course, was never in just one place at any given time. When she was making love to Jara, she was at the same time in, say, the leper colony, hugging a flyblown man swaddled in bandages. She was also in the bedroom with Shastri, filling him in on the details of his native city. 'I was getting the strap of my sandal fixed,' she said. 'The cobbler was lecturing a foreigner on the subtle complexities of Benaras: Benaras is nothing but maya, an illusion; others maintain that it is a construct of smoke, mirrors and fortuitous lighting; and still others are of the opinion that it is composed of memories, dreams, hopes and fears. But the tourist paid no attention to his babble; he was pointing to a dishevelled bird riding on a charred corpse floating down the holy Ganga . . .'

Without a pause she added, 'A new deity complete with smouldering joss sticks has taken up residence between the wrestlers' arena and the dyers' vats . . .' and so they went on, her reports on Benaras.

While she was on a non-stop talking binge with Shastri, she was whipping Jara with her knee-length, silken hair and simultaneously visiting the twisting alleys of the red-light district that came alive only after dark. She gave herself to several people who needed her most, at the same time. One night, after an unseasonal downpour, a cold wind blew in from upriver. And when that happened, Benaras acquired its characteristic smell of truffles and sex. Bitia, who was intent on avoiding a lurching cripple from bumping into her, was grabbed by a dope addict who darted out of the shadows and threw her under a paan-stained, granite staircase into a cobwebbed, mossy corner on some sopping gunnysacks; it was a case of drug overdose. He grabbed her in his wasted arms and threatened to cut her up if she tried to get away. She calmed him down and convinced him to put away his cut-throat razor. He kept repeating the word thirsty like a charm or a prayer. She gathered him in her arms and guided his grinning rictus to her bare breast. He was dying. She was lactating. Bitia, full of grace, cradled his twisted form in her arms long after his body had turned cold. She stayed with him like that until daybreak. One starry winter night, when Bitia was headed towards the hospice for child prostitutes, a deranged hawker of forest-produce lured her down some disused steps, to the shrine of a homemade god next to a septic tank on a sewage landfill. He was so emotionally tortured that she let him lead her away. The place gave off an awful stench. After forcing himself on her, he attempted to ritually sacrifice her by beheading her with his axe but botched it and hung himself with a length of hemp from a dead tree before she could save him.

Leading the nightlife that led her, it was not at all uncommon for Bitia to be beaten, drugged, raped and sodomized by some of the very people whom she succoured. But she bore no scars from these incidents. The more she was battered, the more inviolate she became. As the years went by she steadily grew younger and more beautiful till she was incandescent as a feverish saint. Already there was some loose talk among the pious in the freemason's lodge of the imminence of a second coming or a new avatar. Bitia the ghost passed into the folklore and bazaar gossip of that timeless city of death and desire.

The night was coming to an end. It was a night like any other. Bitia was severally returning home from her bouts of passion and compassion from various parts of the city that never went to sleep. Smoky figures stirred in the last dark of early morning as the first streaks of adamantine light appeared in the eastern sky, when Bitia turned her back on Benaras and disappeared forever, much as she had appeared out of nowhere. The aura she left behind formed the core around which grew the cult of Bitia Devi, the latest in a series of mother goddesses in the subcontinent.

Letter from a Dead Wife

I'd had a sleepless night because of a bad cold. It was only to keep a promise to an old friend that I caught the bus to the club that dusty day. I had hardly entered the club when the fat politician called out to me, 'So you want to go to Guayaquil?'

I looked around. My friend was nowhere in sight. Nobody seemed to have heard the words addressed to me. The various groups of people were busy with their own conversations. A bitch lay on her side in the corner suckling her litter. A goat was tethered to the far end of the counter. The politician was sitting with his sandalled feet hooked to the rings of the bar stool, his dirty dhoti stretched taut like a tent over two sides of his stool. His white kurta seemed too short over his potbelly. His hairy arms on the counter made a circle in which rested his glass of rum, and next to it a packet of paan. He stood out among the others just as much as I, a priest, would be noticeable.

I wear my hair in a tuft. Sacred ash and vermilion mark my forehead. I too wear a dhoti. But my bare torso is diagonally divided by the sacred thread that goes over my left shoulder and beneath my right armpit. With his question echoing in my ears, I thought with vexation that all kinds of unsavoury strangers seemed to know my innermost desires. However, I had a friend to wait for, and then this stranger had accosted me and finally I had nothing to lose so I said, 'Sure,' and sat next to him.

'Why?'

'I like the musical sound of the name,' I said, giving nothing away.

'It'll never come through,' he said. 'You know why?'

'I am listening.'

'Your papers are stuck. Your files cannot move, because you're a priest.'

'Can I do anything about a thing like that?' I asked. 'After all, I am what I am, and nothing can change that.'

'To begin with, you can try being a little less arrogant. Only a politician will be able to pull the right strings and get things moving. I am going to help you. You know why?' He had a trick of ending with a question. I said nothing because I knew he was going to tell me anyway.

'I know you despise me. I know of the nightmare thing that happened to you three years ago. Do not be alarmed. As a politician, it is my business to know these and such other things. I have access. But,' he leaned towards me and his wife leaned towards him, as he whispered, 'it's not just me. Half the people in this place would know your case. The very walls have ears. Ask my wife.' He turned towards her, bumping into her, and she smiled in complete agreement, if not harmony, showing the paan-stained teeth in her red mouth.

'Forget Guayaquil. It is a dead end. Even if you find anything there, it will not bring her back to life though it most certainly will kill something more in you. For three years you have been dying piecemeal until you are only half a man today. Look at you! Your temple is like an abandoned cave, full of bats and spiders. Who prays there? Those who once looked to you for guidance have long turned away from you and even forgotten that there is such a thing as god.'

His voice droned on. I was sleepy and had a splitting headache. I could not any more pay attention to the words that were filtering through to me, even though there was some truth in what he said. The oblongs of yellow sunlight, which came in through the wooden shutters, now lay foreshortened on the peeling wall beyond the sleeping goat. But for all that, the approaching afternoon glare had more than doubled. The audible but unclear conversation all around had an undercurrent of the buzzing of flies much as a drone instrument is played as an accompaniment even during pauses in a musical composition.

My wife knew nothing about music when I first met her. I taught her everything she later came to know and love about music. I may be a priest but my true passion is music, not religion. I think that no prayer, no temple can ever achieve the lofty architecture of a musical composition. Very simply, what happened was this: my wife ran away to Guayaquil with my best, my childhood friend, who was a blind composer. I think of Ashok, even now, as the greatest musician of all time. He was passionately religious, a drunkard, a sadist, and a rabid womanizer. He used to beat his women. Yet so many women threw themselves at him.

We had no children, my wife and I. Our first child was stillborn. Something within my wife broke then. She took to music with a savage intensity. With Ashok, religion was never a matter of ritual; it was an act of faith and total self-surrender.

One day Asha was not there with me any more. I ran to tell Ashok and found him gone. They were seen together at the airport. There were rumours that the two of them had made off to Guayaquil; it was not only another country half a world away, it was another world. When I heard the name Guayaquil, I recalled that when I first met Asha she had once—just the one time—mentioned how Sheeny, her only brother, on discovering that he suffered from leprosy, had fled to distant Guayaquil.

There was no word from Asha and Ashok for a long time. There was no word of them until three years ago when what remained of my mind and world were shattered. It seemed that Ashok had died in Guayaquil and that the people there had forced Asha against her will to be cremated on Ashok's funeral pyre. There was also some loose talk of the ultimate horror: the subduing and cremation of Asha had been recorded on film—a real-life documentary, so to speak.

As if this was not bad enough, even Asha's mother, Amma, who stays with me, had somehow heard of all this. We have never exchanged a word about Asha, between the two of us. But each of us obliquely learns what the other knows, through various things said and unsaid. Both my parents are dead. Now Amma is all I have. Normally she is a person of infinite patience and consideration. But after hearing of Asha's death, Amma has started talking to me about Asha's long-dead father and my non-existent children, her imaginary grandchildren. She is losing her mind, but gracefully. There is nothing bitter or violent about her chatter. She just talks more now—not about the living but only the dead and the unborn. The other day as I came out of the prayer room—I had been praying for rain because of the delayed monsoon—Amma said, 'Don't forget the little one has to be inoculated today. He has to have his booster shot. I spoke to the doctor, he's coming at eleven.'

'Yes, Amma,' I said. Our family doctor knows her case history so it is no problem. Another time as I was stepping out she said, 'When you return could you please get me a jackfruit? Tomorrow is Asha's father's birthday, and I want to surprise him.'

I bought the jackfruit.

I was startled when the politician nudged me out of my reverie. My tepid lemonade stood untouched before me in a puddle of ice-melt. It was obvious my friend was not going to turn up. 'Actually,' the politician said, 'I called you here for a specific purpose.'

'It is not because of you that I came,' I said, crudely rubbing the sleep out of my eyes. 'I came to meet an old friend who has ditched me.'

He waved both his hands in front of his face as though he was clearing cobwebs in the air, in a gesture of dismissal. 'It's a minor matter of no consequence. Moreover . . .'

'Minor matter? You call it a minor matter?'

'Of no consequence. Here,' he said, 'is a letter from your wife. It had been doing the rounds of the various departments until I rescued it for you.' In his hands lay an envelope that had not been tampered with. It had my name and address written in my late wife's unmistakable hand. I tore open the envelope there and then and began to read the letter:

There's no address because I don't want you to write. Don't ask why. Don't ask why I haven't written for so long. You love me. Ashok beats me. You have always treated me (and my mother) with consideration. Ashok uses me like a broom. The difference is, he needs me, you don't. I know I've been unfair, I am not making excuses, but some things one can't explain. It's you I love but here I am with Ashok and here I'll be. Why go into all this uselessly when nothing is made any clearer after the air is cleared of all these words?

Sheeny can't be found. What features do you expect to find when you're looking for a leper? They all look exactly alike. The other thing could be that he never really came to Guayaquil. Anyway I don't want you to think that I came here to look for Sheeny. Tell Amma nothing—she'll only blame me. She'll blame me anyway. I am not trying to say you are to blame. Sorry, I can't go on with the letter like this. I'll just change tack.

This is leper country—a country without mirrors or memories. They have two seasons here: in the summer it rains every other day and in the rainy season, it rains every day. Cyclones are common. The first year we had four. The greenery all round is luxuriant to an unbelievable degree. The lichen-covered trees trail beards of dripping moss. There are creepers and lianas everywhere. The rainforest is all about us. We are really in the dark. The maximum temperature here is about twenty-eight degrees but the humidity is very high. We are not really far from the sea but for all practical purposes it may be a million miles, so impossible are the swamps and the rainforests that barricade us.

When the sky is cloudless, the air is clear and dust free; and in that glare one tends to fall into the illusion that one can see beyond the horizon. This is a slow, sleepy place drowning in the sun and rain where nothing much ever happens. It is light very early in the morning and it adamantly continues till quite late in the evening. The place abounds in snakes, orchids and scorpions. There are lots of birds and clouds of mosquitoes but no crows and no flies. Isn't that funny? The daylight hours are filled with birdsong and bird calls. With the approaching dark, the frogs begin croaking with a whistling sound, such as you've never heard before.

The people here are very funny with strange gods and ununderstandable customs. Not only are there no graven images or holy books, nothing in nature corresponds to their gods but sounds and the intervals of silence between them. Try and conceive of their divinity as constructed entirely of the architectonics of sound without words—music that is its own meaning. It rains all the time. Everything they do is drenched in joy. These people do not know the meaning of words like regret or hope because for them, today is everything. They pass their whole lives away in singing. It's inexplicable. They listen to music as if it can never end. For them, perhaps, it never ends. Leprosy may eat away your features, you may lose your sense of touch and parts of you may feel no pain, but it does not impair your voice or sense of hearing. They understand that. It is little wonder then that their divinity is a construct of sound. This conception of god must have struck a common chord in them. As a people they are wholly innocent. Of course, everyone is flawed and no one can be anything like perfect. They understand that. And what is more, they firmly believe that this life is all there is—no rebirth or afterlife or eternal soul or nonsense like that: the end. And for that very reason you never know what they'll do next. Human voices raised in unison in prayer creates the very god they pray to. Isn't that wonderful? To be steeped in such faith—that alone can explain their corrosive happiness. They hate work. Perhaps because all their prayers are sounds, not words, music is manna to them.

They've taken Ashok to their hearts and see him as a divine manifestation or something. His total lack of vision increases the lustre of his divinity in their eyes. His dark music is their divine illumination. Ashok is ruthless with them and they love it. He satisfies all his appetites at their expense to an inconceivable degree that reaches out beyond life into death. Even their dead are not safe from him. He is not only their high priest but also very nearly one of their gods. He is the only one who is not suspect among the keepers of their faith here.

He loves snakes and now the snakes love me. He garlands my nude body in their writhing coils the better to make love to me in tune to his latest composition. In the beginning, I felt cast aside by his atrocious needs. But I, unlike you, have learned not to be conclusive, judgemental. Ashok cannot see what he is doing. The Eustachian tubes of his ears are filled with a sublime, celestial music. Once he composed a beautiful song for me set to the simple text:

In your eyes I set my sails
Seeing my own sight failing

The harmony, the silence and the resonance-after of his music are not sullied by the slime and mire of his other actions. He cannot even understand that we are both lepers now. I am his foresight, hindsight, second sight, backward glance and stare. When we first came to this house, we found that one side of it was waterlogged. To this day we have been unable to drain it. At the back, on a ber tree, is a macaw which had earlier been a caged pet and, when released, flew away, only to return a few hours later, to its old moorings. It makes a racket the whole day long and keeps stripping the bark of the ber tree. They say there is also a shy monkey on the loose hereabouts though I've never set eyes on him. Further back there is a primary music school for children and behind it is the endless leper colony that is Guayaquil.

In some small ways the lepers are like you: their lives are ruled by compassion and rectitude. They would rather go into hiding than cause a stranger any embarrassment at the sight of their disfigurement. Leprosy erases all features. No individual is unique to behold. All look the same even if they are unique in other ways. In this place the leprous face is every man and woman's permanent mask. There are no mirrors in this country of lepers for the simple reason that to look at anyone's face is to look at your own reflection. They have a saying here that only those wishing to escape or run away from something come to this country. And if somebody follows them in the forlorn hope of finding them, everybody agrees that it must be the ultimate delusion. When I saw the bird that shunned its freedom and returned to its cage, I felt somehow that I had come into my true inheritance. I had looked

> *into the mirror of myself as you had always exhorted me to. So at last I have arrived home after travelling these thousands of miles to the eye of this storm of unknowing and confusion. So be it. The next time you marry, make sure it's a woman who will bear you many children.*

There the letter abruptly ended. It was her hand, her voice. Of that there can be no doubt. I think of that beloved face overlaid with the leonine features common to all lepers with every unique particular erased. No star anywhere can be further from me than you, my love—so far have you moved away from me. I am truly undone.

'Come with me,' the politician says. I follow him. We arrive at the side entrance to one of the ministerial buildings, go down a long corridor, ascend a few floors in an elevator and finally enter a vast room where a few people are waiting for us or for him. Some plates of festive sweets are brought in because, according to the lunar calendar, today commemorates the annual demeaning of a demon by one of the consorts of one of the Hindu gods.

There is a clamouring outside and I step out on to the balcony. There is a central courtyard down below enclosed on three sides by the self-same buildings. Gathered together is a crowd of people yelling. The sight of me appearing on the balcony seems to galvanize them for some reason and they shout all the more. From that height and distance I can recognize quite a few faces: they are all devotees whose ritual prayers I used to perform before they deserted me.

A sudden hush falls over the multitude of my former supplicants because the politician has appeared behind me and made a sign to them. He calls me in. The light in the room has been doused, the furniture rearranged, the drapes drawn and everyone expectant for the screening of a film. I run to the balcony. Behind my back I hear the politician's sarcastic voice: 'So you want to go to Guayaquil?'

Ashok may have been evil, but at least he was human. Asha could see that. But I—I am merely a life-hating priest. With my bare torso I am already half-naked. The only thing left for the crowd to do, when I dive into their midst, is to rend these remaining garments off me and mob my naked body till they and I are one. An unseen woman's recorded voice screams 'Don't' in an unknown language, far away, long ago. It is only the beginning of the film.

Kashi

I have returned to Kashi with Paro, my daughter. I remember a song from my childhood, *'First there was Kashi, then the world'*. Later it was called Benaras. Now it is known as Varanasi. But I grew up here and for me it'll always be Kashi. When I left Kashi for Bombay, I was baffled by the loss of a city which held my lost childhood captive in its mean backstreets.

I know Paro yearns to be back with her old friends in Bombay, the city she grew up in. At eighteen years of age she burns with an intense beauty that was never her mother's when she was young. What young man, I wonder, will not be burnt to a cinder at close contact with that unguarded face? I do not say this because she's my daughter. I do not say this because she is all I have. Like other girls of her age she will marry and leave me. This is as it should be. But I will not have her throw herself away on some riff-raff. When my wife deserted us, I said to myself, had the child been a boy or I the mother, things would have been different. Were I not a schoolmaster, with a daughter on my hands, I would have managed things better, more easily. I had got into the habit of arguing with myself. I don't as yet talk aloud to myself. Perhaps that too will happen. I used to keep telling myself these and similar things in such a way and to such an extent that I began to accept that things were as they were. Did I find new arguments to shift part of the burden off my shoulders and so comfort myself? Yes, yes. At any rate, those days I endlessly talked about these things to myself . . .

I have returned to Kashi, this city of the dead and the dying. Not because I wanted to revisit the scenes of my childhood or find easy access to the town's nightlife which I frequent out of boredom and which can hardly have more to offer than Bombay's red-light district, but because there seemed nowhere else to go. My wife suddenly turned up in Bombay, with a young man, after a twelve-year absence, and wanted to meet me in the teachers' common room after school hours. I stared at them with the chalky fingers of my hands knitted in anger: my wife looked younger than I remembered and had the same helpless look, while the youth wore the face of a liar. She still had that break in her defenceless voice. I glared at her in silence. I was not taken in any more by the beauty of her forlorn and deceitful fragility. She was a practising prostitute when I married her, against the combined opposition of my parents and all the relatives of the extended family. How could I then let them meet my Paro? Only my two friends stood by me: one of them is dead and the other (which amounts to the same thing) has emigrated to America. I have not mentioned a word of all this to Paro. And so we came to Kashi, this many-layered city of cities.

Like all sinners, I have returned to this city of lights. Young people come here to learn Sanskrit and study the Vedas. Pilgrims come here to pray; seers and sages to preach. Householders bring the cremated ashes of deceased relations to Kashi so as to commit them to the waters of the Ganga at their holiest. Renouncers and devotees come here to visit ashrams, temples, retreats, hermitages, shrines and pavilions; widows who have nowhere else to go come here out of piety, while the bereft and the abused hurry here due to the sheer pressure of misery. Beggars seeking alms congregate in Kashi because it is here that the faithful are expected to give of their plenty. The infirm and the terminal come here to die. Kashi is different things to different people.

My afternoons are free and I often take a walk down the shady side of the twisting streets; winters, I sit out in the sun and read *Sport & Pastime*. Mornings, I teach at the Boys Normal School and evenings, I hold special classes in non-formal adult education for which I've set apart a room in my house. I have the middle of the day all to myself as Paro goes off to the library directly after college and returns home only when I am taking my evening classes. I notice that we don't speak much to each other. Sometimes these special night-school classes are held in different parts of the city to enable those without any means of conveyance to attend them. On such and other nights Paro has a cup of hot tea ready for me when I enter the house, with my bicycle clips in one hand and the attendance register in the other. Sometimes she even helps me out with the maps and charts at the evening classes at home. She has the vulnerable beauty of her mother's eyes; and her voice has a catch in it—a kind of breathlessness—that breaks my heart every time I hear it.

I've observed her on many a Sunday morning, after a head bath, drying her long black hair at the window with a faraway look in her eyes as she absently gazes at the cycle-rickshaws clattering by and the pariah dogs prowling the streets; the vehicles move around the collapsed bull as if it is a traffic island; the open gutters stream past the paan-stained walls of the wrestling arenas into the holy river. But Paro's heart and mind are in Bombay. I never disturb her at such moments and take great care never to be caught watching her. But I know that look in her eyes though she does not say a word to me—she misses the big city, the seaside and her old friends. Here, you can see the half-burnt bodies of the dead floating down the luminous river of life with a crow perched on a limb or torso, pecking away at the flesh that has been abandoned by the spirit, which has already made the great crossing to the farther shore. The river banks at Kashi are crowded with beggars and believers. You don't have to beg or believe to walk among them. You are never part of the scene you see. And so it is with Paro. She longs for the lights of Bombay, its fast traffic and electric trains, and its magic anonymity of belonging to something that can never, in turn, belong to you. If she wants to return to Bombay, I shall have to tell her about the incident in the school. But she says nothing and I don't explain.

One day I am offered the deputy-headship of the school. The following afternoon, just after the first rains, as I walk westward through the municipal gardens past Gadaulia, I suddenly find myself behind the house I grew up in as a boy, looking down on it from a back street which is almost level with the roofs of row upon row of similar houses, several of them grouped into each compound. I don't remember them being here at all. Probably because it has rained all last night the air vibrates with an aching clarity, bathing everything in a dream-like light. It is the same old pile all right. Through the open doors of the hall I can see the jasmine bush on the front veranda, the open passage leading down to the central courtyard with the kitchen and lavatory on either side of the cowshed, the well in the centre, and beside it the lemon tree whose branches overhang the unprotected staircase leading up to the four rooms opening into each other. My ancestral house is not located here at all. It's all wrong. My memory seems to be playing tricks on me. I grew up in an eastern suburb of Kashi. At all costs I must guard against the rising damp in my mind.

But my surprise at finding myself before my old home, or at finding it here, is nothing compared to the shock of seeing Paro leave the house through a side entrance and delicately make her way through the rubbish-strewn, narrow passage (where I played marbles as a child) towards the street that leads to town. I draw back involuntarily though I know that it is quite impossible for her to see me. Paro. My Paro.

It begins to drizzle and I don't know by what route I make my way back home through the maze of narrow gullies with their sewage drains, hedged in, tier upon tier, by the crooked buildings with their sagging balconies displaying the day's washing hung out to dry above the shops selling silk brocade, brass utensils and pure ghee, and steps everywhere going up or down turning poky streets into precarious staircases. I only remember that as I'm leaving the place, the children in a neighbouring school are singing that maddening song, '*First there was Kashi, then the world*'. I retreat in wild confusion, my hands clapped to my ears.

Paro is not at home when I get back. There is an unopened envelope with the seal of the chairman of the school board waiting for me—it must be the formal letter informing me of my promotion. The first of my students, Srinivasan, an old man with a wheezing cough who comes in every day, is already waiting for me. I let the letter lie unopened. We nod at each other in greeting.

As I towel my head dry I think that he comes to me for consolation, not education, for his stupidity is matched only by his regularity in attendance and his complaints about his emphysema. His lungs have long since lost their elasticity, he tells me; he seems to be waiting, after his fashion, for the end. There are worse places to die in than Kashi—even for a reprobate like myself. He will learn nothing here even if he continues to hound me all my life.

'Let me see your copybook, please,' I say.

I give all my attention to Srinivasan for I do not want to think about Paro. I leaf through the blank pages; his rough-book is full of weak attempts at lewd drawings.

Poor devil! He used to be an itinerant quack performing cataract operations with a thorn on the eyes of unsuspecting villagers till the law caught up with him. He has a large family to support. And after the law caught up with him for the third time, he set himself up as a faith-healer. He attends my classes only because the probationary officers injunct him to do so. In his studies he is exceptionally dense and in his work he must be—ailing as he is—the worst advertisement for his healing prowess, faith or no faith.

None of my other students come in and Srinivasan is fidgeting as if he would rather be elsewhere.

'Srinivasan,' I say, 'I know why you have to attend these

classes. But as I've said before, you'll learn nothing here. I have promised to mark you present when you are absent and yet you turn up at all the night-school classes. You are the most regular even if the worst student in all of Kashi. It's a mystery to me.'

'I'll be frank with you,' he says. 'I'll be as frank with you as you have been with me. I'm not the man you take me for. I come to you simply because I've nowhere else to go. And now,' he says, getting to his feet, 'you'll have to excuse me. The other students have not turned up and will not turn up tonight. And I don't want to end up by saying things to you I should not as yet mention.'

I must somehow detain him. Even more, I'm intrigued and alarmed by his words and not untouched by his modest attempt at honesty.

'What is it that you cannot bring yourself to mention now to me?' I ask. I almost smile, in spite of myself, at these words.

'Would you recognize your master if you met him in the street?' he asks.

I must admit I'm quite unprepared for this. I cannot help grinning. 'Are you referring to my teacher or my maker?'

'It's nothing,' he mumbles and fussily gets out of the way of Paro who's at the door.

I had, however briefly, forgotten all about Paro. 'Don't go!' I cry, even though I don't want to see him any more, but he is gone and Paro holds my brown outstretched hand in both her own. The sudden contact—it is like in the old days when I used to take her for walks as a child, just after her mother had left us—and suddenly I realize that Paro has become the compass by which I take the bearings of my godless life.

'Father,' says Paro, leading me into the next room, 'I want you to meet Ashok.'

An abridged edition of that layabout Srinivasan. I look into the lying face of the young man standing before me, avoiding my eyes, much as he had stood before me all those years ago, with my wife by his side, in the school in Bombay.

'But Paro, he's a liar!' I almost say, but just in time I bite my tongue bringing tears to my eyes.

I see now that my wife is there sitting on the sofa. And so are a lot of others, among them my paan-stained aunt and asthmatic uncle from Ghazipur, whom I've not seen in years.

If I look closely at the people gathered here I'm sure I should recognize all my old relations. But I don't have the time. And what is that idiot Srinivasan doing here? It is clear that they have met without me and have arrived at decisions that are now going to be put to me as accomplished facts. Who are these people and what are they to me? Where were they when I needed them? I never wanted them to meet my daughter. And because I want no part of them I turn to Paro. I pull her back against the blackboard in the next room. My tone when I speak to her, though, is gentle. 'Paro, why have you deceived me?'

There is already the promise of tears in her voice when she says, 'Father, you really must not give way to the feeling that I've betrayed you just because I want you to meet Ashok. One moment you are a god and the next you doubt your very manhood. But look around you, father, sometimes. The world is changing. Where are you?'

I must remember to ask her what she was doing at the old

ancestral house earlier in the day. But the pace and pressure of my anxieties are such that the question escapes me the instant it enters my head. 'My child,' I say instead, 'I saw your mother with Ashok before you ever brought him to meet me.'

'It's a lie,' she cries, running out of the room.

Has somebody been talking to her about her mother's past? I see her whole future fading into her parent's past. The lying manipulators! Without upsetting Paro I must teach them a lesson they will not forget. I'm not to be had in this way.

I return to the room and address my daughter who is standing, already composed, alone in a corner: 'Is this Ashok the man you want to marry, Parvati?' I ask, formally but clearly, in the sudden well of silence that my voice has created for itself amidst these wretched people.

She hangs her head in the unmistakable sign of shy assent and tears flow down her cheeks.

'All right, my child,' I say, and there are smiles all round and a general hubbub, as though I have played my part exactly as they had arranged it for me. I turn my back on all that useless chatter and set out towards my childhood home where it all began. My life is a shambles now. I lose my way, retrace my steps and go through the municipal gardens, past Gadaulia . . . but it's no use. It's raining again. I must return home. But the house is nowhere to be seen. I rudely brush past an acquaintance with a new umbrella who stops me under a street lamp to exchange an amiable word or two.

My life here is finished. Why do I feel that what is happening to me here, now, is something I'll never wake up from? I stand here, in the pouring rain, my life wasted, amidst the wreckage of my broken dreams and the falling debris of my shattered hopes. I accept my weaknesses, I admit all my failures. I console myself that this can happen to anyone anywhere: Uttarkashi in the north, Sivakashi in the south or just about any suburb of Kashi to the east or west of Gadaulia, say. Full of resolution I take a taxi and give directions to take me to the house situated on the other side of town as I remember it from childhood. And there in an eastern suburb of Kashi it stands, exactly as I remember it, but now heavily decorated with lights and festooned with streamers, bunting, tinsel and paper-lanterns; the lemon tree is decorated with small, winking lights. The lintels over the threshold and windows are hung with mango leaves; the cow and calf, their foreheads daubed with auspicious vermilion, are tethered in front of the house, with a petromax gas-lamp for company.

As I enter the house, I already know what I'll find. I'm now ready to accept whatever is decided for me.

They are all there—all the people I had turned away from at home. Ashok's father, Srinivasan—how could I have missed it earlier—ushers me into the room and introduces me to a bald, spare, nondescript man in ochre robes who smiles and speaks to me in the kindest tone: 'My brother,' he says, as though he is continuing the conversation that he left off with Srinivasan, 'teaching, believing and learning have nothing to do with faith. It's only doing. Let me show you. You'll not regret it. Not for one moment.'

This is mere pious nonsense but I now have nothing to lose and do not argue, for I too now want to be taught the things that one never learns. I follow him out but turn back at the door to have one last look at these people: Paro is crying and next to her Ashok is at a loss, not knowing how to comfort her. Everybody is downcast including my wife, as though things are going against their deepest desires. There is a smell of festive cooking in the air but the atmosphere is so heavy with gloom that I'm happy to leave them behind and follow this stranger. The sky has cleared and the breeze is picking up. In the cold moonlight I am made to sit on the stone steps of the ghats going down to the river and my head is shaved bald. After a dip in the dirty waters I'm smeared with sandalwood paste, anointed with holy oil and my forehead is marked with sacred ash and vermilion. I have returned to Kashi for this and this only.

I cast off my old clothes and instead receive two lengths of ochre cloth: one goes around my loins and the other is draped over my shivering shoulders; and in the weak light of the false dawn I start walking barefoot, with the new companion who is to accompany me—he is young, mute, with a ready smile. First the Bishwanath Temple, then the Manikarnika Kund, and then south along the banks of the Ganga as far as the Assi Ghat, followed by prayers at the Durga Temple and so on to the Panchkosi Road, towards Kardameshwar, Bhimchadi, Rameshwar, Kapildhara, the Barna Sangam and so back to Manikarnika. The monsoon has started in earnest. I keep fasts, pray in Sanskrit, a language I do not know, and give alms from my share of the food. I bathe in the river every day and invariably do as my brethren do. Time does not matter. To begin with, I had to faithlessly repeat the words I never understood. The hours and years go by undifferentiated from each other in one continuous flow. Here, in time, misery teaches even unbelievers how to keep the faith. That is why saints have sung in praise of Kashi, the city older than history, which has existed long before time began and will be there long after the end of time. By Ganga here I have laid down my burden in the holy city, eternal Kashi. Am I happy? Am I sad? May as well ask, am I alive? You beg, you believe, you belong.

In the Wake

One morning Ambaal walked into the bedroom and saw her husband's lifeless body sprawled on her side of the double bed. She found it impossible to accept the sight before her unbelieving eyes. Ambaal was returning home from a meeting of a non-governmental organization in Gurgaon that had dragged on all night.

Her husband was wearing her peach-coloured bras and panties and his fingernails like his lips were painted blood red. The cheeks were heavily rouged, the eyebrows picked out in a dark pencil and the scant eyelashes thickly mascaraed. The eyelids were touched up in pink and highlighted with glitter. His mane of grey hair was combed right back and parted in the middle. The violently painted mouth had fallen open and the lipstick smudged in a tiny arc on one side suggested a smirk, as if the massive overdose of sleeping pills was a private and final joke. One eye was closed in a wicked wink. Over all this, there was the traditional sandalwood-paste caste-mark on his forehead.

Ambaal's necklaces adorned his neck where the foundation

make-up came to a marked end. His arms were heavy with her bangles. He had chosen only those items of jewellery which his own parents had given Ambaal at the time of their marriage, long years ago.

The sacred thread ran diagonally down the bare left shoulder across his hirsute torso and between the deflated cups of the lacy bras. One hairy testicle had slipped out from under the edging at the groin of the panties. His toenails like his fingernails were painted red, and on his feet he wore Ambaal's favourite party sandals with platform cork heels. The sleeping pills had left his face looking relaxed, almost serene.

To Ambaal, her husband's body, tricked out in her under things, ornaments and paints, presented a hideous spectacle that, in one instant, made a mockery and a shambles of her life. The social rectitude, the strict adherence to the accepted codes of piety and community, the active submission to Brahminical restraint and to the cultural hierarchies of her fellow-beings—these and several other small and large worldly considerations that had gone into the making of her shared life with her husband now lay shattered into shards all around her. The significance of her dead husband lying there like a painted slut refused to find acceptance in her horrified eyes for quite some time. Was this the man she had shared her whole life with all these years? What would the others say? She was paralysed with revulsion. She stood staring at her husband's corpse for quite a while before ringing up the police. When they answered her call, she was unable to say a word. They traced her through the live, open telephone line. The servant was absconding. Waves of nausea and fatigue wracked her slender frame as she sat on a sofa in the drawing room.

The house was steeped in silence except for the monotonous sound of a single voice talking to itself. It issued from the mouth of an old woman in the third room down the corridor: it was Ambaal's mother-in-law. She was going over some memory that had recently been lit up by the neurons firing in some part of her peevish head. She would repeat the story endlessly without pause until the spittle in her mouth ran dry or a new memory replaced the old one between the synapses of her flickering past. She repeated the story like a circular mantra without beginning or end: 'I returned from Gaya yesterday. The floods have been heavy this year. I called a meeting of the doctors. So many boats have capsized in the river. Some bodies washed ashore but most of them washed away. Untraceable. Terrible, terrible. People being brought to the hospital where they were declared brought dead. The water levels rising everywhere. When I met the queen, they told me it was her birthday and I said, a happy birthday to you and many happy returns and she said, thank you and I said welcome and the others were taken aback and asked why did you do that and I said it was only natural as it was her birthday and they said but she is the queen and I said so what? I told the doctors to move all the patients and medical stores from the ground floor and distribute them on the first, second and third floors. I have been away so long in Bettiah that I do not recognize a single street here. Everything here has changed. Not at all like Bettiah where nothing changes; I just returned from Gaya yesterday. The floods have been heavy this year. I called a meeting . . .'

Named Brihadhambaal at birth, Ambaal grew up with her three sisters and a brother in Pudukkotai. After school and college, her marriage had been arranged, with quiet pride, to Thindivanam Dhakshinamurthy Shankarnarayanan (Shanky to his co-labourers in the Indian Administrative Service). His people came from Kumbakonam. His father was a senior judge in the Patna High Court and his mother was one of the first lady doctors and gynaecologists to practise in Patna and then in Bettiah in north Bihar. Shanky was an only child and much was expected of him. Passing the I.A.S. was the full flowering of that promise. This merely meant that he was a good catch in the marriage market.

Ambaal's own father was a schoolteacher who took private tuitions to supplement his modest income. Though the times were not exactly easy, it had been a happy enough childhood divided, as in all such households, between studies, play and singing lessons. Hopscotch, ludo, hide-and-seek, seven-tiles and kho-kho were the great favourites. When Ambaal had been married, two of her sisters, Chupputai and Meenakshi, died of typhoid within four days of each other. Indereshan, her brother, studying in the ninth standard in the local school where his father taught, ran away from home. He could not be traced and his mother, unable to escape the domino effect of the accumulating losses, went over the edge and committed suicide by throwing herself into the well in the backyard of their house in the dead of night. Ambaal's father lost his job because he simply could not continue with his teaching; his tuitions dried up. Ambaal's third sister, Rajalakshmi, became a seamstress in Mayavaram, where she settled down with her ailing father in reduced circumstances.

At the time of Ambaal's marriage, Shanky's family astrologer had consulted other astrologers. Their horoscopes were particularly well-matched, they said: the ascendant constellations in the appropriate houses, the transits with reference to the original moon signs, particularly the harmony in the seventh house, the suitable positions of both Mars and Venus—everything, in short, confirmed a long, happy and fruitful marriage unmarred by any scandalous denouement. There had not been even the barest hint of humiliation or tragedy; and now this.

There was the whiff of scandal surrounding Shanky's suicide. There was talk that all those related to Ambaal were fated to suffer and die in desperate circumstances. Astrologers were quoted, omens were read and almanacs studied to buttress their bogus claims. To add an element of zest, some of the more venturesome among the trouble-mongers started the practice of sighting Ambaal's missing brother, Indereshan, doing odd jobs in odd places: he was seen hawking fuel in Madurai; selling paan in Madanapalli; slinking into a mosque in Kuttanallur; and vending meat in Thoothukodi. The ineffectuality of these piquant rumours turned it into a callous game and the authors started going farther and farther away: Indereshan was sighted smuggling wetbacks across the Mexican border, pimping in Amsterdam and cooking on a container ship in Costa Rica.

Shanky's body was cleaned up and smeared with sandalwood paste and clarified butter. A new white dhoti covered Shanky from waist to ankle. The torso was bare. His nostrils and ears were stuffed with cotton wool dipped in holy oil. The eyes were closed shut. A bandage went over his head and under his jaws to keep the mouth closed. His two big toes were tied together with string. The body was laid out on a bamboo ladder that was placed on the wet floor of the drawing room. It was strewn with flowers—mostly marigolds. The furniture in the room had all been pushed to the walls, leaving the middle bare. The carpet had been removed. The windows were thrown open. The main door leading to the outside as well as the two doors leading to the two wings of the house were kept wide open. The air was heavy with smoke and the chanting of the three priests, one of whom was going round the body sprinkling water on it with a tuft of darbha grass in one hand which he dipped into a copper pot that he held in the other.

All the women in the household stood around dripping and shivering. Buckets of water had been emptied over each of the women by the servants at the bidding of the chief priest. The feet of the corpse faced the main entrance to the hall.

The three professional mourners were howling outside where the sacred fire had been lit on the ground. No one had summoned them. They had found their way to the house of death in exactly the same mysterious way as hermaphrodites are said to find their way to a home where a male infant is born. The mourners were three elderly women in white blouses and saris, their hair hanging loose down their backs. They beat their breasts rhythmically and cried their eyes out, wailing for the departed. It was as though the loss was not only personal but intimate.

The four men who were to carry the body came loping into the hall. They were a shocking sight: dog-like, with furry limbs and strangely twisted hindquarters. The secondary priest came in swinging a smoking pot in a string cradle that he dandled and dangled as if it were a cross between an infant and an incense burner.

Summoned by a mixture of envy and the scent of scandal

in high places, relations from far and near started gratuitously pouring in to assist in the obsequies and condole with the bereaved. There was Athimbair, Ambaal's late cousin's husband from Tranquebar. Then there was Sapna, her nephew's uppity wife from Coimbatore. Her own ageing uncle and aunt—exact replicas of her neighbours at the window across the street—from their crumbling house in the Brahmin street in the village near Darmapuram. Ambaal's husband's cousin and his son, both wastrels from Matunga in Mumbai and, of course, her own two daughters and their respective husbands, smooth young computer engineers who were patiently waiting for their green cards. There were others—close as well as distant relations—but Ambaal had eyes only for her third child and only son, Ishan, who had arrived from America just that morning. She had Ishan's horoscope cast by the most expensive astrologer in Delhi; she was sure she would find the best girl for him in the not-too-distant future. How tall he had grown; his shoulders and chest had filled out; his longish hair, combed wet earlier, was now attractively dishevelled. Perhaps he looked as he did because his carefree face—particularly the eyes—his whole carriage, in fact, seemed to point towards some inner emptiness.

Surrounded by the din, the crowds, the garlands, the ritual chanting of Sanskrit prayers, the incense, the smoke and the gossip, Ishan was quite lost. It was already well into summer and he who had got quite unused to the heat found it stunning. His jet-lagged mind returned again and again, like a tongue to a gum-boil, to his leave-taking in America. Pakeeza had not cried, and he, the bereaved, had no words of comfort for her. Like most people from the subcontinent—

she from Pakistan and he from India—they were serious about their relationship without its becoming overly physical. They had been going out with each other for over a year now and were committed to each other, though neither of them had said it in so many words. Unlike him, however, Pakeeza was possessed of both grace and courage—qualities quite alien to his temperament. They stood outside the airport, as she wanted to finish the cigarette she was smoking. They stood together in silence with his luggage, looking for all the world like a pair of punished schoolchildren in a classroom corner. Neither of them wanted to be the first to speak, though both were aware that the time for departure was approaching. In lieu of something to say, perhaps, Pakeeza lit another cigarette with the butt of the last one. She had smoked and he had taken in the air until it was time for them to separate. I'll write, she had said, as he had reached out and touched her shoulders with the tips of his fingers and silently mouthed the words, take care now.

There was one moment in that bustle and noise when Ambaal stopped to stare at the group of beggars crying for alms outside the gate. A slender, bearded figure at the back of the crowd looked exactly like her missing brother, Indereshan. Just then, somebody called out to her and when she turned back towards the group of beggars, the face she was looking for was missing. She went up to the gate and looked down both sides of the street in vain. She returned to the house, her head bent with the palm of her right hand against her forehead for she suddenly feared that she was in real danger of losing her mind.

The menfolk accompanied the body to the crematorium where a cement platform had been prepared under a corrugated asbestos roof supported on four cast-iron girders. As ritually demanded by religious tradition, the corpse made its entry into the cremation grounds feet first. The priest with the pot of fire hanging from a cat's cradle led the procession into the crematorium as the last stragglers from a previous funeral were leaving the place.

Split logs of wood were laid in a criss-cross pattern on the cement platform on which the body was placed. The eyes, nose, mouth, forehead and biceps of the corpse were sprinkled with holy water and anointed with sacred ash, oil and sandalwood paste. A few grains of raw rice and one rupee coins were placed on the eyes and in the palm of each hand; the arms were tied to the sides of the body with coir rope. The priests kept up their chanting of Sanskrit prayers.

The split logs of wood were placed all around and over the body, leaving only the chest bare and uncovered. The clayey soil moistened with water was made into a dough-like paste and plastered over the whole wooden construct with the body enclosed in it, leaving only the chest area bare. Ishan was made to perambulate around the body seven times. The priest with the pot of fire came forward and offered the pot to Ishan who emptied it on the chest of his dead father as he was instructed. The mourners returned home to cleanse themselves with their ritual baths. The four creatures who had carried the body were left behind to keep vigil and see to it that the fire did not go out, as the body at the end of its earthly journey in this life was committed to a slow burn.

It was the day after the funeral. Ishan, who had briefly dozed off, awoke with a start and checked his pocket where he was carrying his father's cremated ashes in a plastic pouch. The bus was going up a mountain road in the second gear, making a great racket as it slowly progressed. Ishan had vetoed the idea of going by car. The elbow poking into Ishan's side belonged to an elderly man who was making faces at no one in particular.

The dust storm was at its worst and the bus was forced to make several unscheduled halts as the visibility was down to near zero. It was one of those freakish storms. There were the terrible sounds of thunder and flashes of lightning lit up the entire dust-laden sky. Some of the children in the bus began howling inconsolably. 'What a lousy time to make a pilgrimage,' said the old man sitting next to him. 'At the rate at which we are going, I think there's a good chance that we'll all be dead before we even reach our destination. I wonder if we have not left this for too late.'

Ishan smiled non-committally. He was carrying his father's cremated ashes for ritual immersion as per the wishes of the elders in the family. The bus was moving again but only in second gear, negotiating the treacherous hairpin bends and the sudden ascents and descents of the mountain roads. The old man turned his contorted face towards Ishan and said, 'It's my dentures. They are loose and hurt something terrible.'

Ishan nodded sympathetically. That explained the old man's twitching face. When the bus stopped, the conductor informed them that they were running late due to the electric storm; the passengers were encouraged to get out of the bus to stretch their legs and have a cup of tea to refresh themselves. In answer to a question, he said that they would not reach their destination before nightfall. The mountain air was thin and chilly. The tea stall was perched on the edge of a rock over the gorge and seemed to extend into the failing twilight. While drinking his tea, Ishan noticed that the outside of the bus was streaked with vomit from the windows, and caked over with dust.

Suddenly it began to rain and all the people rushed into the bus. Just as the last stragglers got in, it began to hail. The hailstones fell with a clatter on the baggage piled on the roof of the bus. The ravens that had been flying around just a few minutes ago had disappeared.

As the bus slowly made its way through the hailstorm, Ishan looked out of the window, at the repetitively ever-changing scene outside. Just before he dozed off, he turned towards the old man sitting next to him. He seemed to have aged another thirty years or so. His cheeks caved in, his watery eyes shut, and his lips pouting like the mouth of a purse whose drawstrings have been pulled tight. He glanced at his lap and saw that the man was holding his dentures cupped in his hands.

The bus suddenly stopped. The driver turned and announced that they had reached their destination. The storm was over. The cold sky was full of stars. In the dark, even the rest house where they were to stay was barely visible. The caretaker was there to receive them. 'Please hurry up now,' he hustled them. 'It's already very late. And all of you must be ready to leave for the cliff-temple at five o'clock in the morning. That means you have only four hours to rest.'

There was no sign of the cliff-temple, no sound from the vast concourse of pilgrims. Tired and beaten, the passengers picked up their baggage as the driver and conductor of the bus handed them their suitcases and bags from the windy roof of the bus. The caretaker showed him to his room. It was a narrow room with a low cast-iron cot and a pedestal lamp by its side. The lamp had no shade and the door had no latch. The caretaker pushed his bag farther into the room with his foot and asked, 'Would you like to meet my younger sister? She has just come from the village.'

'No,' said Ishan, 'and shut the door after you, please.'

He reached out to the switch and put out the pedestal lamp, plunging the room into darkness, when the door opened and there was a chilly draft of air.

'I am the caretaker's sister,' she said, in the darkness, as she shut the door behind her. She gave off the smell of raw cut onions and for a moment Ishan was afraid she would bring tears to his eyes. Ishan reached out and put on the light the better to look at the girl. She was a hill girl, in her teens, with the complexion and features of the hill people: fair with full lips, blunt features and straight black hair. He moved his legs on the bed to his side and made a place for her to sit.

'Please, no light,' she said, and Ishan switched out the light a second time. In the dark, the girl settled on the bed and Ishan could feel the warmth from her body seep into his legs through the cotton quilt.

'Are you really his sister?' Ishan asked, thinking he could see no connection between this girl sitting next to him in the dark and the wizened man who had showed him to this room.

'In our village,' she said, 'on the other side of the valley, everybody believes that he is my brother. I too say he is my brother just as he says I am his sister.'

'You know, nobody would guess you two could be brother and sister,' said Ishan. 'He looks so old and you are so young.'

She giggled and crept into bed with him under the quilt. She must have spread her shawl on the quilt for Ishan suddenly felt a delicious sense of warmth invade his body;

there was, at the same time, the smell of poverty and raw onions. Ishan had never been this close to a woman in this way, and he was quite at sea. She sensed his hesitation and confidently took over. Obviously, she was experienced, in spite of her age. Their lovemaking was all over in no time at all and Ishan rolled off her on to his side of the bed, breathing heavily. So, this was it. The mystery was not solved. If anything, it had deepened and Ishan felt quite let down. The girl next to him made a low noise at the base of her throat as she coaxed him to come on her again.

'Will you come down to the plains with me?' Ishan asked her.

'No.'

'Why?'

'I'll get bored,' she said. 'Here, I sleep the whole day and at night I get to meet different people, mostly those going on a pilgrimage like you. From my village across the valley, I came to this place. Here I meet people from all over the world, and when they enter me, I travel through them to the distant parts of the globe where they come from. I feel I see things differently because I travel through different people. People come here to pray and wash off all their sins. Good people who make me feel good. That is why I don't ever want to leave this place or get married in the village. Here I'll never grow old, renewing myself every night as I travel vast distances to return exhausted by morning to this sleeping body.'

'I would like to live with you,' said Ishan. 'If you don't want to come down to the plains with me, maybe I can stay here in the hills with you?'

'They all want to be with me,' she said with a little laugh, giving his cheek an affectionate pinch. 'And you are no different. Of course, you can't stay here with me. Just see that old caretaker who goes around telling everyone that he's my brother. He too was young once, like you. Just look at what's happened to him, now that he stays here with me. After sleeping with me, he begged me to allow him to stay on here with me even if only as a brother. I gave in when I couldn't stand his pleading any more. And what's the result? He has become as old as the hills. He'll pop it any day now, the rate at which he's going. You are young and have your whole life before you. Don't throw it away on these windy hills. So many wasted lives are scattered hereabouts already. I have my life to lead in these hills and here I'll stay but I suggest that you go about your business as usual with daybreak. You think your heart is broken. But soon, all too soon, you'll think of this as a dream—as something that never really happened.'

'Let me stay here as your brother, nightly conducting you to other men in other rooms. You yourself said just now that the old man is going to die. Let me take his place and be your brother.'

'How many brothers can I accommodate? No. You'll have to leave, for the present at any rate. You can think of these things after he's gone, maybe. But not now.'

'All right,' said Ishan, nearly pushing her out of the bed. 'If that's the way you feel about things, then leave now.'

'Hey, take it easy,' she said. 'Only a minute ago you wanted to spend your whole life with me, and here you are, kicking me out of your bed.'

'You better go now,' said Ishan to the girl, who was laughing. 'I must get up early in the morning and sort out the millions of things I have to do. In any case, I don't see why I have to behave towards you as though you were a part of my life when we both know and have agreed that we have to go our separate ways.'

She only laughed and snuggled closer to him under the quilt. Her voice when she next spoke to him was coy and muffled by the quilt. 'So you want to stay here with me?' she said.

'No,' said Ishan. 'Much as I would like to, I just can't stay here. There are things that need doing and my presence is absolutely necessary elsewhere.'

''Then I can come down to the plains with you. That way you can get your work done and we can both be together,' she said, popping her head out of the quilt.

'If you do that,' he said, 'you'll always feel that you've given up your way of life for an unknown mode of being. It would be the foundation of a life-long regret. And then what is one to say to your ageing brother here? We can't just dump him and run away together. No. All things considered, it is best that you stay here with him and lead the life you are leading and I shall return to the old ways of my life.'

'But he cares nothing for me,' she said. 'And anyway, I care absolutely nothing for him. Also, I am getting tired of his hangdog look, as though I belong to him and as though everything I do takes him one step closer to his funeral pyre. I want to get out of here.'

'You said you travelled the whole world with those you spent the night with. You said you never wanted to exchange that indiscriminate variety for the dull predictability of marriage. Anyway, it'll be morning soon and sunlight has a way of sorting out these things. We'll see things in a different light then. Go to sleep now.'

She accepted his word and went to sleep. He too fell into a dreamless sleep of exhaustion. The moment Ishan dropped off to sleep, the girl woke up and gently got out of bed. She took from his wallet the exact amount of money earlier agreed upon. As she left the room and closed the door behind her, she could hear the first stirrings of the day coming from the common kitchen downstairs. It was still dark and she easily avoided the shaft of light coming from the kitchen doorway on to the staircase landing below as she pulled her shawl tightly about her shoulders and slipped out into the early morning darkness outside.

The caretaker woke Ishan up by standing at the open door and shouting, 'Wake up, wake up.' Ishan hurried through his ablutions and came down with his bag packed and ready. Some of the others were at breakfast in the large central hall. The old man with dentures waved rather extravagantly to him and Ishan went and sat next to him after depositing his bag at the side of his chair. Breakfast was broken-wheat porridge with milk and sugar and curried potatoes with puris. The old man asked him if he had slept well and without waiting for an answer, dived into his milky porridge. He ate slowly and with evident relish, making strange slurping noises probably occasioned by his loose dentures.

After breakfast everybody drifted one by one to the bus outside. The caretaker was nowhere in sight. Nor was the girl to be seen anywhere but that was only natural as the daylight hours were her sleeping time. The bus had been washed clean in last night's downpour. The day was fresh and the still air smelled of wet grass and shrubbery. Soon the bus was full and the driver and conductor appeared, as chief guests at a public function will, at the last minute; and they were off on the last leg of their sacred journey. In barely two hours time the bus came rattling to a halt at the black granite cliff-face of the mountaintop into which a series of steps had been cut with nailed ropes above to provide a handhold. It gave every appearance of being a dangerous enterprise. From where the pilgrims stood, they could see people going up but no one coming down. The devotees made their way down a different route on the other side of the hill. Most of the people left their personal belongings in the bus except for the few essential items that they needed to take with them in the holy ascent to the summit where the consecrated source of the holy river awaited them.

The climb to the top was not as difficult as it looked. In fact, it was surprisingly easy. There, on the top, he saw the old man in tears, his face shrunken and drawn. Before Ishan could say a word, the old man blurted out his story. 'While coming up I sneezed and my dentures flew right out of my mouth into the abyss below. I don't know what I'll do now,' he wailed.

'Anyway,' said Ishan, to console him, 'they never did fit you well. Now you can get yourself another pair of dentures that will fit you better and not give you any trouble.'

'You don't understand,' the old man wailed. 'Those dentures were not mine, but my dead wife's. It was the only keepsake that she had left me.'

The entrance to the cave was narrow and confined, allowing passage for only one person at a time. There was the strong ammonia stench of bat guano in the cave, made the more unbearable with the smells of human sweat and burning oil. The route past the dark deity and the source of the sacred river turned abruptly to the right, went up a narrow, rock-hewn staircase that continued steeply up until it suddenly broke into the sunshine outside. From here the devotees descended the cliff by a route laid for them on the southern side of the mountain. Behind the stone deity, surrounded by oil lamps in the sanctum sanctorum, there gurgled from a hole in the rock a tiny spring of fresh water that flowed out of the temple cave. It came down the other side of the mountain—one of the largest rivers in the world—to wend its way over two thousand miles of mountainous terrain, rainforests, swamps and long stretches of plains until it reached the sea. It was considered most auspicious that the ashes of a dead person should be consigned to this river, preferably at its very source.

Ishan prostrated himself before the deity, opened the plastic pouch, and committed his father's ashes to the spring of fresh water. He turned around and saw that the old man was now far behind. The distance between Ishan and the other pilgrims had grown considerably. Ishan spread out his hands on either side of himself in his ascent through the dark staircase as if he were doing a balancing act.

When he stepped out into the bright sunlight, the most unbelievable sight met his eyes: the caretaker and his sister, who were wrestling each other silently just ahead, fell down the sheer cliff-face over the low railing without a cry. Ishan rushed to the spot where they had been grappling each other, and looked over the edge into the void. There was nothing to see. Ishan looked around the bend to see if anybody else was there who had gone ahead of him. There was nobody there. The last of those who had preceded him were making their way down, quite some distance away. Ishan rushed back, but neither the toothless old man nor any of the others had as yet emerged from the darkness of the sacred cave below. Shaken, Ishan made his way to safety.

When later Ishan mentioned what he had seen to the others, they nodded their heads in sympathy and made clucking noises. They understood, they said. These things happen, they said. What else do you expect? It was always just like this, they said. Back at the rest house there was no sign of the caretaker or his sister. Another man who was filling in as a substitute for the old caretaker told him that the old chap had left early that morning for his village across the valley to attend some religious festival. The man was young and dressed in a khaki uniform of some sort. He came from another village, he said, not the same one as the old caretaker. 'That is just a village of pimps and prostitutes,' he said, with evident contempt.

When Ishan asked about the old caretaker's sister, he just laughed and flapped his hands dismissively. 'But,' he said, 'If you are planning to stay the night here in the rest house, you can meet my sister who will be coming here later in the evening to join me.'

Ishan turned and fled to the bus, which was just preparing to leave for the plains with its load of pious devotees. Quite bewildered with the entire funeral-pilgrimage, Ishan made his way back to Delhi, en route to America, as in a dream. While still in a daze, his grandmother pressed sweetmeats on him and told him her old story: 'The queen has been heavy this year and I said many happy returns to the monsoons in Gaya because the patients were swimming and the doctors drowned in the streets of Bettiah', and so on.

Before Ishan returned from his pilgrimage, there was a letter for him from America. Ambaal, with ill-bred possessiveness, had torn open the envelope and read the beautiful letter from Pakeeza with vulgar avidity.

My dear Ishan,

Your absence here is telling. The days are empty and endless. I have not been working as well as I should have and old Dr Kowalski is angry with me. He asked me to see the student counsellor—that dimpled baldy—if I had any emotional problems that came in the way of my work. I lied to him. I told him that it was a temporary medical problem, for which I was already receiving treatment.

Waheedha left for Karachi and Saskia is hunting around for somebody who will share the room with her. Like you, Waheedha too had to leave suddenly, only I don't know the reason why. Saskia says she's sure Waheedha will not return. I saw four movies with W before she suddenly upped and left without a word to me. One Vietnamese movie, The Scent of Green Papaya, *I want to see again with you when you are back here. I am sure you'll love it.*

There was a letter from my mother asking me to come back. Then there was a similar letter from my brother and then a third letter from—hold your breath—my father's first wife (Badi Ammi), in Urdu: quite a sweet letter ending with a couplet asking me to return home to my roots. None of the letters give any reasons and all of them are long on nostalgia. I am convinced it has to do with their marriage plans for me. No matter how 'modern' or 'progressive' our people may wish to be, at heart they are all traditionalists. I am not against nostalgia and sentiment—I am, in fact, all for it. But I have not replied to any one of the three letters.

In fact, after your departure and the arrival of the three letters I mentioned, I've been assailed by numberless images of the home country. Particularly before I fall asleep, when

I cannot be said to be either awake or asleep, I see, as in a reverie, images of the Lahore cantonment area where I grew up. It was formerly a British residential district of wide, tree-lined avenues with crumbling white bungalows set in large, shady gardens; there is a ruined church beside the derelict Christian cemetery. I remember the gymkhana club, the cricket grounds, the shopping arcades along the mall, the Canal Bank Road running alongside the canal with lush greenery on both sides all the way from Jallo Park to Thokkar Niaz Baig. I can almost smell the walled city with the faded elegance of its bazaars, where men in colourful turbans brush their teeth with strips of walnut bark (much as you said people in your country use neem twigs) lounging under tarpaulin awnings flapping in the wind over mounds of sticky sweet dates, and the camel and donkey carts jostling each other in the narrow alleyways with the hawkers crying out their wares . . . But above all else I recall a childhood trip with my grandmother to her ancestral home in Quetta: the hillsides carpeted with wild, red and yellow tulips being cleared for the cultivation of saffron, the whole place spilling over with almonds, apricots, apples, pomegranates, peaches, plums, pistachios . . . I suppose I mention all this to you at such length not because I long to return home but because I've quite made up my mind, and I want you to know it, that I shall never return to Pakistan.

You notice I've deliberately held myself back from asking how things are with you in India. I long to hear these things from you in person and in the meanwhile I'd love to hear from you as to when you plan to be back here. I've given up saying my prayers. Just as my love for you has

made me turn my back (you are not responsible for this) on my country, so too has my concern for the primacy of things human made me faithless to my god and religion.
As ever, Pakeeza.

Ambaal read the letter through two more times before locking it up next to Ishan's horoscope in her jewellery box, her mind firmly made up that this was not a letter Ishan should ever see. What kind of a girl was this? No respect for her parents or authority. No love for her land and her people. Ready to turn her back on God and religion—chee, chee—even the biggest bribe to an astrologer could not fix a horoscope for such a she-devil. Some weeks after Shanky's funeral and Ishan's return to America, a pair of used panties and a bra were stuffed into the mailbox nailed to Ambaal's garden gate. Ambaal resisted the pressures of local calumny and decided to get back into social circulation as a way of finally putting her husband's death behind her. But sorrow is its own country and Ambaal, a stranger in this new landscape, found herself hemmed in, every so often, just when she thought she would break through. During the sleepless hours that now regularly visited her for the greater part of each night, she searched in vain for a way out.

Her sleepless nights were followed by headaches that dogged her in the daytime. She retreated to her heavily curtained room, smeared her forehead with some balm, and lay down with wads of wet towels on her eyes and head. During her intermittent reveries she dreamt of old houses in Daryaganj, the old quarter of the walled city where she had started her married life when she first came to Delhi: bungalows with courtyards, twisting alleys with their open drains, the jangle of cycle-rickshaws and the periodic cries of hawkers. She saw in her dream picture the large, permanently locked gate in the compound wall with the smaller pedestrian gate let into it and permanently kept open. There were many houses inside, around the common, central courtyard open to the sky. The rooms in those old buildings had high ceilings with dusty skylights that let in the soft light and the slatted wooden windows that shuttered the interiors against the afternoon glare. The naked bulbs hung by wires from the rafters and there were cobwebs in secret corners, dark and cool in the daytime heat. She could smell the creamy smells of the frangipani seeping in under the locked doors. She could hear the distant cries of vendors going about their business. She dreamt of the calm of the innermost room of the dream house as though these composite images from her married past held a secret cure to her present problems.

Her menstrual periods became irregular and a single, horrible hair surfaced on her left nipple, as though it stood for everything that was obnoxious in life. Soon the hours of darkness became hours of argument: she would discuss with herself in endless and pointless detail every aspect of her unravelling life.

The family doctor prescribed tranquillizers that kept her awake and gave her double vision. About Shanky, he encouraged her to think back over their past life for any anomalous behaviour on Shanky's part, not necessarily related to cross-dressing. So the days went by. It was the second half of the long, hot summer. Ambaal closed her eyes and saw against her rosy eyelids the dry riverbed dotted with watermelons growing in the vast sandy stretches interspersed with distant puddles of filthy water with flyblown buffaloes wallowing in them. The air over the burning sands was quick with dragonflies and midges. Kites and other scavenging birds wheeled over the old garbage dump hunting for thermals on the banks of the once sweet Jamuna. Tufts of grass were a rarity, parched to the stalk in the scorching noonday sun; the trees were camel coloured with dust. Wherever one happened to be, one saw smoke rising in the distance from burning litter or rubbish. The traffic roared endlessly along the melting tar roads, which gave off a shimmering haze. The pinched figures on the earthen verge of the asphalt roads wobbled in the glassy glaze of the heat. Ambaal lay cocooned in her darkened room as if felled by the humming air-conditioner. Try as she might, she could not bring herself to examine Shanky's past. Her mind would wander or switch off. These repeated failures left her more exhausted than ever.

A Brahmin priest, recommended by a friend of a friend, suggested that she try and pay the minutest attention to the coming on of the headache; to watch out for signals if any; note the timings and follow it step by step as it grew to its full size and occupied her whole being. The doctor said that she should be keenly aware of the whole process from start to finish. But Ambaal could not keep her mind on the painful process as it tended to stray and wander. She felt a degree of relief in letting go of her teetering mind and watching it with another part of herself as though she were two different people at once. The priest suggested that she stay on course with the images that had the most calming effect on her. The image that soothed her the most was that of the sacred river. She followed it from its source in the granite cave in the mountains, taking in the other streams and rivulets fed by the snowmelt that joined it; its turbulent youth among boulders and down waterfalls; its gathering power and size at the foothills as it cut deeper and deeper channels through the rocks and ate up vast chunks of land on either bank. Middle age in the riparian lowlands put the breaks on its swift passage and the river grew deep and sluggish, meandering and curving towards its final estuarial apotheosis in the sea, thousands of miles away from its modest beginnings in the black rock cliffs. In some part of herself, deep within, Ambaal unconsciously saw herself hurtling towards some kind of a fall she could not pull out of.

Ambaal began dreaming in her sleep and remembering her dreams on waking up. This left her with the feeling that she had not slept well or at all. To begin with, there were the dreams of flying, falling and snakes; then came the dreams of her own funeral. The flower-strewn body on the bamboo ladder placed on the floor was her own. At the same time she was standing, wet and shivering beside it, alongside the others, observing the proceedings, much as she had done not so long ago at Shanky's funeral.

'So you are the dreamer who dreams that she is attending the funeral where she herself is the deceased?' the latest doctor asked.

'Yes,' she said. 'But also I see my own missing brother, who I am sure I had a fleeting glance of, at my husband's funeral.'

'Significant,' said the doctor. 'But still and all, it is a mere detail.'

'I know the people who are standing next to me but the moment I turn to them, each one in turn becomes a blank cut-out.' She paused and then went on quickly, 'Whatever all this may mean, doctor, I feel lonely and exhausted. There are people around me. Yet I am completely alone. In effect, I fear I may do myself some irreparable harm for I have been increasingly feeling of late that nothing, but nothing, is worth my while any more. Help me doctor, please, I think something terrible is going to happen to me.'

The next day, the servant found Ambaal dead when he went in to inform her that there was a visitor from the NGO in Gurgaon waiting to see her. Ambaal was hanging from the ceiling fan dressed in her husband's clothes. Her long hair was cut short and cropped like a man. The face was mottled purple with the congealed blood and the features were crunched together unrecognizably. She wore no make-up or jewellery. Even the pierced ear lobes were gaping empty. Her forehead was unmarked by the customary vermilion. Her short hair was heavily gelled and parted, not in the middle as usual but on the side. Her bulging eyeballs started out of her congealed face. Her open mouth was stopped with her black, swollen tongue. Her neck was at an angle to the body because of the noose, fashioned from her husband's suspenders. She wore her husband's clothes: shirt, tie, jacket and trousers—all far too big for her. The trousers were held up at the waist by the belt, which had passed through the loops of the trousers but was tied into an awkward knot in the front probably because there were no appropriate holes for the buckle to fasten it to. The bottoms of the trousers were rolled up several times, one more than the other. Her hands had disappeared into the long sleeves of the shirt and jacket, just the tips of a digit or two peeped out of the cuffs held together by her husband's favourite cufflinks, which he reserved for formal social occasions. The heels of both socks had ridden up to the ankles. One shoe had fallen to the ground near the leg of the fallen stool while the other precariously hung on. Her own clothes were nowhere to be seen. The switch of her long hair, severed from her head, lay in a wastebasket, alongside Pakeeza's old letter, now torn to shreds. The body hung nearly motionless in the breathless room. In another room of the same house, Ambaal's mother-in-law's voice droned on, '. . . when the queen was washed ashore yesterday in Bettiah, I said happy birthday to the drowned patients in the upper floors of the hospital where the flood waters were rising because the doctors were distributing dead bodies to the river boats . . .'

Ex-votos for a Mask Maker

The story is of course false to itself, including these very words, but Ishan Kara had got used to telling himself that it must be told. When you come to tell this story, if at all, to another, please remember this lie among all the other lies, and remember also, that it will further change in the telling.

Ishan could not write any more.

Before he had come to the end of himself, he had written four plays. The last play, *Ex-votos for a Mask Maker*, completed three years ago, had been repeatedly rehearsed, but never staged. As was his usual practice, Ishan incorporated into the play the changes suggested during rehearsals by the members of the cast and the director. The general feeling, shared by Ishan, was that at the heart of the play, as in his other plays, there remained a certain residuum which eluded depiction on stage.

The play, a farce in three acts, depicts a short-story writer at the height of his powers contemplating on an afternoon his just completed handiwork, when the fictional figures of his story actually enter his room and call his work (the story of a playwright who is put to death by the players he has gathered around him) into question, before killing him. The writing of *Ex-votos for a Mask Maker* had given Ishan no reason to believe that he was drying up; ironically, Ishan had often asked himself in the past, 'Who can tell what form one's going away will take?' This feeling persisted, in spite of the open-endedness of the play which clearly foretold the author's death (a piece of useless knowledge shared by Ishan, with all the rest); in spite of the songs that had their necessary place in the play; in spite of the fully formed characters and the markedly uncluttered structure of their relations with each other in the play; in spite of the suggested modifications which had since become part of the play; and in spite of so much else.

In fact, the members of the original cast, including Ishan, had gone north to Madurai with the play. There is a picture taken there on Ishan's thirty-third birthday showing them standing in a row before a temple tank. There is no water to be seen though some people in the middle distance can be seen washing their clothes.

All of them are young, but only Vidya in the flowered sari and Srinivasan whose hand is bandaged are smiling. Ishan's head is bowed down as though by the weight of his horn-rimmed spectacles and Vasant is holding Alka's hand and looking directly into the camera—Ashok's camera.

Denzil looks lost and Ashraf is talking to Gapli, the prettiest girl in the group: in fact, her beauty was such that her face, her memorable face, wore the look of not wanting to be remembered by anyone. Tari, Jitin and Yogi are only partially visible and Anil is staring into the bowl of his pipe. Vicky's bearded face is a grey blur.

For various reasons the rehearsals were abandoned after this picture was taken and the play was never put on the boards. After their return home, Ishan had lied to himself about some trivial matter—a minor abuse of language that masked an act of self-deception.

When he sat down to write that evening, Ishan found himself up against a kind of difficulty so different from any he had ever encountered till then as to be a totally new experience. Accustomed as he was to forgetting himself at such times, he suddenly found that thoughts about himself kept obtruding into his conscious mind at the moment of composition. It was as though what he put into writing, while becoming concrete, at the same time moved into a false relationship with him. Ishan conversed continuously with the characters he could not bring to life and over the days and months the voices of the living and dead masters, that had gone into the making of his own voice, receded into the distance, became indistinct and finally fell silent. Other voices invaded his head—the familiar voices of the characters he had created in *Ex-votos for a Mask Maker*. Vidya's voice said, 'You believed in the actuality of your own play and invested it with reality to such an extent that even if it rang untrue to the whole world, for you it is true enough to kill you.'

Denzil said, 'When you created us you put into our hands the instruments of your own destruction. The density of your overwrought words has played havoc with our lives. We have played all subsequent parts with you behind and before us.' Srinivasan complained, 'It is true you assigned me a role. But the incomplete characterization has caused me great embarrassment: only a part of me acts while the other part is forced to be satisfied with the contemplation of the acting of the first part and, clearly, the fault is yours.' And Ashok said, 'Through the years as each role bypassed me, I thought that each of them in turn was meant for me. Your problem is, you wait too long. But because of you I have no role of my own to play and I do not know who I am.' Jitin said, 'You abandoned us. But all our lives lay in the direction of your will when you suddenly chose to be silent and so locked us eternally into this half-existence. We could do only one thing: and that is, wait for you. But you will never write again.' 'There is no hope for us now. We will have to enact your end according to your own script to find our release,' whispered Gapli as she bit his ear. A strange voice said, 'We have come as envoys from, if you like, your past life. We have brought with us your songs of yesterday. Do you remember the hill stations in the off-season? And the songs they played all day long around the skating rink?'

Alka sang:

We like to believe the rains will let up
But then
The muddy eddy of after-rain
Whirls the leaves of our longings
Down the bed of a dry-wash
Of shale and stone that choke
Their flow to reality and our hopes
Remain longings and the long evenings
Single before a doused fire
Stifles desire and waters
The seeds of our discontent.

There was so much Ishan wanted to say. It was important he say it now. Exactly for that reason, perhaps, he could say nothing. Each of them said their say before biting Ishan who bled defencelessly. He could feel the contained breathing of unseen presences expectantly pressing down upon the lower lighted area from the upper reaches of darkness in the room. He could hear Lila and Joachim talking to each other in stage whispers. The room itself was assembled from discarded settings, spent stage properties and outdated advertisement hoardings. Ashraf retreated towards the others who took their ease with nonchalance among the litter of stage properties and became indistinguishable from them. Carefully disposed at random lounged the figures he had yet to look at. Impossible to tell how many there were—excessively relaxed and theatrically silent. Ishan strained his eyes and gazed into the dusty half-light of their faces. Were they perhaps characters from his earlier plays, rehearsing the lines of some other playwright who now held sway over them?'

In their eyes he saw their past and his future. 'It is as I had thought,' said Ishan to himself, 'I am now closer home.'

The voices all spoke on cue as though from the farthest distance and at the same time close to his ear, and not one spoke out of turn except when they were to overlap for effect to suit their vague words to their apposite actions. 'Do you know why you'll never write again?' asked Anil and Vasant answered, wiping his mouth, 'Because you cannot see the dark shapes that lie behind all words.'

'Yes,' said somebody else. 'Yes. You lied to yourself and so let the night into your work. There is just too much darkness there. And you are nothing but your work, your words.' Vicky said, 'Crowded by words you became immune to them.'

'You are silent now,' said an unfamiliar figure, 'because the words will not come to you.' Tari said, 'How forgetful you are of what you yourself once fashioned with your whole being, to encompass your own selfish ends!'

Yogi said, 'With you living we are only half-beings. Better, far better, that we were nothing and you were dead.'

A voice from the shadows said, 'It is only the lies that we tell ourselves that count. You know that. We could go on like this forever but there is no point in it. Besides, even you . . .'

An unknown voice cut in, 'Ishan. Above all, do not delude yourself that you have lied to yourself about some trivial matter, that the whole thing is a mere matter of semantics or a minor abuse of language.' They had quite bitten him to death by now and the blood had formed a puddle round his feet. The last words Ishan heard were whispered into his bleeding mouth: 'You are dying of the terrible beauty of your writing, Ishan, because you cannot believe in your own words any more. Whatever anyone else might say, you have lost all faith in us. Now and forever more, do not expect anyone to believe what you yourself do not believe in.' Self-absorbed, before Ishan's flickering eyes, each of them wiped the total make-up off their faces, and changed from their costumes into their street clothes; among them he saw or thought he recognized Iona, Sujit and Karim. Released from all pain he dozed off and dreamt of his childhood as they drove him out of the city in the pre-dawn darkness. He could hear the temple bells ringing across the paddy fields of his sleepy village as he had set out in search, it seemed, of this very story with its mofussil beginnings which would be completed only by his death, in the city's garbage dump.

What a long haul it has been, thought Ishan. He felt no pain at all when he was thrown on the refuse heap and they stood about him ankle-deep in the filth, disoriented, unrelated to one another—unfamiliar, in fact, to one another, severed from all commonality of purpose, and suddenly aged beyond their years they shambled away, their task completed.

Streaks of obstinate light appeared in the eastern sky. The crows had gathered under each doused streetlight along the Grand Trunk Highway leading out of the city, drawn there by the myriads of dead insects crushed by the lorries of the night. A bulldozer and two tractors lay idle among the garbage dunes of the sanitary landfill that made up the undulating line of the horizon; in the middle distance ragged women and children were rummaging among the smoking heaps of refuse dumped by the red-and-grey municipal trucks. The tourists clustered around the air-conditioned bus that had stopped at the octroi checkpost four miles outside the city limits, near the hot-mix plant, and seventeen miles from the inter-state bus depot. The guide had to dissuade one of the tourists who wanted to photograph, at close quarters, the numberless kites, vultures and crows circling over and hopping amidst the smoking hillocks of rubbish.

The slow smoke from the ash pits and the smouldering refuse around him rose gently into the still morning sky of early summer. Ignoring the ants and vermin that were at him, Ishan began to tell himself the story, as one who knew only too well that no story has a beginning or end, up to and including the point at which he began to tell himself the story: the story was of course false to itself . . .

Acknowledgements

All the characters in my fiction are, at least in part, some of the many people that I am—I who am nothing but a construct of my obligations to other people. This life is a shapeless thing of borrowed bits and stolen voices; only stories seem to have any form. There are so many to whom I owe so much, who I will never know personally because these dead masters belonged to other times and other places and sometimes wrote in other languages. And then there are those, some of whom may never read this, but for whom you would not be reading this. To name all of them, to apportion my gratitude and love to each of them in a suitable measure would be beyond my feeble means. I may not however gloss over in silence those who were close to me. Some of them are no more. They are, in no particular order: Anil Mashruwalla, Syed M. Ashraf, Avtar K. (Tari) Gupta, Athmanathan (Atmu) Mani, Denzil Steed, Geetam Tiwari, Vidya Borooah, Anjana (Gapli) Gupta Behal, Raj K. Aggarwala, Jitin Desai, Vani (Vicky) Borooah, T.V. Krishnan, Vasant Kothari, Abhijit Chatterjee, Kajal Das, Dinesh Mohan and Partha Chatterjee. I am grateful to others for several things like their yarns and mottoes that have entered the coarse weave of this threadbare tapestry.

Some of these stories that have grown old with me, minus a few variations, first appeared in the publications against which they are mentioned; grateful acknowledgement is made to these periodicals/anthologies:

'Not to be Loose Shunted': *Stand*, Newcastle-upon-Tyne, England; reproduced in the Sahitya Akademi's *Contemporary Indian Short Stories in English*, New Delhi.

'The Light, The Way': *Imprint*, Mumbai; reproduced in *Namaste*, New Delhi.

'Kashi': *Katha Prize Stories*, Volume 1, New Delhi.

'Letter from a Dead Wife' appeared under the title 'The Music of Leprosy': *India International Centre Quarterly*, New Delhi.

'Ex-votos for a Mask Maker': *Helix* and *Luna*, Australia.

About the Author

Ashok Srinivasan was born seventy years ago in a village in Thanjavur in south India. His novel, *Once Upon a Time*, a savage fairytale for adults, is being readied for press.